TELL ME WHAT YOU SEE

TELL ME WHAT YOU SEE

TERENA ELIZABETH BELL

VT & NYC

WHISKEY TIT

Published in the United States and Canada by Whisk(e)y Tit: www.whiskeytit.com. If you wish to use or reproduce all or part of this book for any means, please let the author and publisher know. You're pretty much required to, legally.

ISBN 978-1-952600-22-7

Contents

WELCOME, FRIEND

The refrigerator door is open, that's the first thing you notice —
and not for cleaning either — It's opened ajar as if a person or the
ghost of a person still stood there casually deciding what to take
for dinner: shelves overflowing with white wine and sandwich
meat sliced, fruits and fancy cheeses, all in a state of decay; The
inside of the refrigerator is blue — there's that much mold: blue
and brown and green and maybe even a little black, dots and
spirals out of control like tendrils reaching — reaching across
walls and shelves and even the refrigerator's sides in a wave —
It's coming for you, whatever this is, and for a moment you think
about slamming the door.

(You have on your gloves; It'd be safe?)

You are not a detective: You never worked for CSI, FBI, no
association with three-letter names where they could have
trained you to work with these things but still — you've seen
enough police procedurals, made-for-tv crime to know

> never touch the scene
> do not alter it
> do not clean it
> do not change one single thing

until you understand what happened — until the truth is
evidence collected, fact and proof, story assembled then told —
You know better than to touch a scene.

These shows, these movies, they belong to before — the Before

---

the something, the Before the nothing, or sometimes just Before; but either way you move along.

You do not shut the door even if the stench is overwhelming, so overwhelming you wonder if it will keep you from discovering real clues, if scent — if smell — were how all this began: the Something, the Nothing made of odors both innocent and maleficent; if smells — all smell, any smell — could tell you how or where they went, then the stench coming out of that refrigerator right now would keep you from ever knowing, take all other smells over and you would die; sweat and breath and pheromones — everything that made you gone: gone like the people who lived here before and then you would never know (were there other people in the world? were you still a person? have you disappeared? — You will not shut the door.)

You go forward toward the living room now.

You're not quite sure what you expected — This isn't the first time you've done a home inspection like this — each job a little different — a pause, a feeling, en medias res, life continuing gone: sometimes it's guitars left out of their cases picks rattling inside, record needles butting the end of 45's; books left open, letters not signed; evidence of life, life everywhere.

There's an almost storybook quality to it, the empty space — or so you've trained yourself to believe — like King Arthur's court, Ramandu's table, maybe they're all asleep; maybe the people are asleep; except, they're not here— There's nobody here just like there was no body at the last place and the place before that and every place before it and all you can find are empty shells — all you can see is the Gone (remnants and belongings and — again with that smell: sure it's a refrigerator here but at the last place it was cat fur and tomorrow it'll be an unflushed commode and no matter how long you go, no matter how long you move among

things trying to find their people, it will never smell like death —
They aren't dead they're just gone.)

THE FIFTH FEAR

First Tome

Amanda's breasts were shriveled, almost dripping, hanging from her body like an old lady's. This was the first thing — the only thing — Tara noticed when her friend came out of the portal. But before she could ask, Amanda covered them with a towel and the man at the gate shouted "go go go," the line moving ever forward, Tara's brother starting to step up and Tara couldn't leave him, oh no she couldn't leave him, and then she looked back — over her shoulder, away from the square — to see Amanda was gone.

*****

The first time Tara went to the portal — not through the portal, rather to the portal — she had not been alone. She was with Amanda.

They'd been to that place in Hell's Kitchen, the Italian one on 11th and West 43rd. The sun was shining and Amanda wanted to see it, watch it set, because "when do we ever go down to the water" so then they went and saw it. No one was there, no people — just me, only the portal and its stairs.

"I'm afraid," Tara said, reaching her fingers into space, the birth of the very first fear. "Don't be silly," Amanda told her, reaching out for Tara's hand.

*****

All fears are the same fear — the truth if you know it and by golly Amanda would know it — but what Tara did not yet know was that I, Douglas Merritte[1], will long know it. I have and will encapsulate fear, absorb the   fear, plug it with my birth at the portal.

In the early days of psychophysical development — one might say its birth — Dr. Karl Albrecht[2] theorized there were only five fears : everything allkind was afraid of — men, women, other, every being in existence that thought they were unique; each thought they had their own fears (plagues, traumas, pasts) — they all thought together that fear was unique but it wasn't
                    // 2004, the birth of the five fears collective :

Extinction
                    defined by Merriam-Webster as "the act of
                    making extinct or causing to be
                    extinguished" : in other words to bring to an
                    end, make an end of

1.
Born March 1, 2020, **Douglas Merritte is** a psychophysicist working across the years 1847, 2357, and 9. From 1918 to 1347, he will also stand guard at the portal.

In a statement to authorities the night she planted the bomb — the bomb that rock out the staircase, the stairs Tara did not notice had started going black while she and her brother stood in line (she did not see the lights descend, did not notice authorities as they cut off the line, bodies moving faster, the guard shouted "go," handing Tara and her brother their suits) — **Merritte's mother said she named him after a child who'd gone missing** [her child who was born in the portal].

"I was there when Amanda went in but couldn't stop her," Merritte told these same authorities March 13, 2143, his mother having already shared the story of his name, her skin sagging down with his absence, Merritte's existence her placenta, her breasts. "She didn't mean to set the bomb, she wanted the bomb unmade."

2.
It was Albrecht who wrote THE FIVE FEARS but Merritte who refined them, who collected them down to one.

Mutilation

> an act or instance of damage or alteration beyond repair : "The readaption of the 60 minute hour into a period of 59 minutes and 13 seconds was the very first time mutilation, some might say" — to use the word in a sentence

Loss of Autonomy

> the fear dissettling allkind as they stood before the portal[3], all other fears single words — the fear of autonomy itself lexically disautonomous, unable to stand on its own, lacking statement, a will, a way

Separation

> the act or the process of separating, the state of being separated itself[4]

[Redacted]

> [While THE FIFTH FEAR certainly alludes to five fears' existence, the identity — or autonomy, if you will — of this last and final fear has slipped from allkind's knowledge]

*****

Tara was afraid of heights, that was the first thing, her brother Nathan saying for the one hundredth time "just don't look down" — as if that ever solved the problem.

3.
They only let people through in pairs.

4.
The strength of portal cannot be born alone.

If the fear of falling could be eradicated by a simple gaze, by a matter of where one placed the eyes, Tara would be climbing. She would scale the tallest building, hang on the Empire State, reach higher and higher, eyes to the skies.

No, looking down was not the issue. Rather it was the complete lack of security — "even trapeze artists have a net," she told the man guarding the portal : this baby, a child, I at the gate. "You're telling me if I fall, there's nothing down there?"

They were at the head of the line, next to go in, and that's when Amanda came out, water dripping all over the platform, down from her breasts, her hair, and when Tara leaned over, she could see it, could see the hollowness that was the portal, holes cutting down through life : the Hudson, the mesh, the Statue of Liberty crying, weeping at the bottom of the world, Amanda's breasts her tears. "Don't you feel vulnerable?" she asked, "What happens if my tether breaks?"

"Then you fall," Nathan laughed, and I said,

"They don't break."

*****

Second Tome

In the age of information, Amanda and Tara were young — and the idea of compressed life times, of having to stretch through a portal in order to live, well, all that seemed rather silly, they were living right now. "It's ignoring the inevitable," Tara said, putting her menu down, "all those people passing through that thing? That's the exact same attitude that got us in this boat" — *this boat* : a society on dark water, far from the shore and sinking.

The flyers were all over town, it was obnoxious — the M11, the subway, the M17 :

LOSE YOURSELF IN THE BEYOND.

LIVE ONE LIFE TIME INSIDE OF MANY.

"People will never go for it," Amanda said, but then of course she went for it, went for it and didn't tell Tara that she would go, exiting the portal, eyes dilated and glazed[5], wiping herself down with a towel — and that's when she saw Tara. She saw Tara and turned, started to say something but did not, then before she had a chance, before Tara could say "you went," before Amanda could say "don't go," it was over. It was Tara and Nathan's turn next in line and they stepped up to the portal. Tara looked through

---

5.

The flyers promise you will not get old. There's not time to grow old in the portal, the portal built to last two weeks, but one week past the portal is one month at the portal is one year for New York on Pause, and to quote Douglas Merritte, "Isn't that just like a dream : a broken promise? And the loss of this promise, the mutilation of id itself ?"

the mesh — but wait : This story will get ahead of itself. (That happens when one mutilates time.)

*****

You stepped through the portal. You stepped out of time. You stepped through and lived life in a dream. And it was a dream in the sense that you did things and thought things and went about things with no cognizance of how much time [but it isn't really a dream it is life and you'll stay until life is finished], then when it was over, when finally it was through — when you were done with it or it was done with you — you will go back again. You step across the portal and time continues : in much smaller increments than you dreamed.

*****

"We've lived with disease for years," Tara told Amanda, back at the Italian place (hours waiting for a table), "Why now," wanting to say she'd seen the numbers, had seen the science and the numbers and thought they're not that bad, "Why are people so afraid now?" then that night they found it, that was the night Amanda had wanted to see the sun set.

*****

Third Tome

one minute past the portal is one hour at the portal is one day
twelve minutes past the portal is twelve hours at the portal is
twelve days one minute past the portal is one hour at the portal
is twelve nights three minutes past the portal is three hours at the
portal is four days one minute past the portal is one hour at the
portal is one day three minutes at the portal is four hours in the
portal is one minute past the portal is one day[6].

** * * *

6.
In the womb, his mother's womb, Douglas Merritte was a child.

Fourth Tome

I was born past the portal, in labor at its gate, conceived on the upper west side. I am made of foam and water, made before the foam and water, the darkening black on this now present side[7].

Through the portal, there is lightness:

> an absence of responsibility, born free of all fears, your responsibility is only to others —

> My mother, she passed through with me inside her : Amanda going in, Amanda setting out, Amanda always dripping.

When Tara and Nathan came through, she was afraid. She'd not yet discovered the single fear you see. She did not yet know

---

7.
In the ripples of what was once Pier 90 on the city's upper west, there lay the quantum foam.

 "The quantum foam is everywhere," said a scientist named Stephen Hawking, once a child now dead, who spoke through a machine : "This is where wormholes exist. Tiny tunnels or shortcuts through space and time; they constantly form, disappear, and reform within this quantum foam — linking two separate places and two different times."

 "Time flows like a river," Hawking told me.

exactly what there was to be afraid of — extinction, separation , redacted sense of self — she did not know every fear was one. To have one fear was to have them all. Every fear is one.

They are absorbed together. They are encapsulated in my body at the portal. They roll like the bodies of those who fell / fall through the mesh :

> The tether breaks. It always breaks. It is the eyes. It's the eyes that keep us from falling, that rise every body to the top, the ever present summit of time.

> **LOSE YOUR** SELF IN THE BEYOND

> LIVE **ONE LIFE** TIME INSIDE OF MANY

Their eyes were not set on the heights, you see. Their eyes are not set, they look down[8].

Standing at the portal, I see them. They step through. There is a hole, an opening (now see!), between this world and that and the trick is to move. You must keep going ever keep going keep going keep going   just move   keep going keep going now always keep going   keep going keep going just move.

This, Nathan told Tara when she yearned to look down, Tara always afraid of heights

> // mutilation — no, extinction.

I've never stepped through the portal myself as Douglas Merritte,

---

8.
Fear drives them to the portal and it keeps them past the portal. Look down at your fear and you drown.

I exist on all sides), but I've seen enough people do it. You simply come through the light :

Dilation

> the act or the process of dilating, the state of being dilated itself : at first, the pupils contract, 4 to 8 mm restricting to half, then focus. Slowly so slowly, both pupils focus to a size beyond your control (Nathan was right, it's all where you look — "focus, Tara, focus" — and then she looked down, saw Liberty beneath her, Manhattan not rising, weeping out of control — millions and millions, they fall through the mesh — Nathan said "take my hand")

Expulsion

> the act of expelling or being expelled : there is no tentative movement; you have to keep going, just ever keep going, until … When you see the light you're not yet in the light — you are on the very first side. You live in the world, the living world, within but without space time. Then you lean. The eyes dilate and the body, the body it goes with the eyes. The spirit it goes with the eyes. So you lean. It is through this leaning — the lean is the portal — that you either fall or rise. Either way you will transition. Either way you are expelled. The moment you look is the moment you pass : the minute, the hour you change

Placental

> the act of pure autonomy, the product of having been expelled : you are out, through the portal, in the after; a transference of

**vascular organs, mind and body adjust to
surroundings** — New York before the portal :
gone.[9]

★****

We cannot go back to conception, we can't make the portal
unmade :

time now passed — exploded.

★****

9.
"But still," Tara asked, "at some point, don't we all have to go back?"

Fifth Tome

[Tomes 1-4 Long Redacted]

When Tara stepped through for the very first time — Amanda now dead, mesh forgotten — she saw trees. She saw trees and mountains she'd never yet seen, as if nature had grown over the island. Ahead, her brother was climbing. "Come on," he now told her, "we're free."

#CORONALIFE

Direct Message from April Mitchell
Mar 9 – 5:15 PM
OMG MAGGIE ARE YOU OKAY?

Direct Message to April Mitchell
Mar 9 – 6:29 PM
April, hey, nice to hear from you.
Thanks for checking in.

Direct Message from April Mitchell
Mar 9 – 6:29 PM
Youre alive!!!!!

Direct Message to April Mitchell
Mar 9 – 6:32 PM
Yeah. Any particular reason I wouldn't be?

Direct Message from April Mitchell
Mar 9 – 6:33 PM
OMG you live in NYC I thought you would have heard
They said on the news ya'll have the rona up there

Direct Message to April Mitchell
Mar 9 – 6:45 PM
Yeah, I'm okay. New York's a big city. 21 people's not a lot.
Appreciate your checking.

Mar 9 – 6:49 PM
How are you?

Direct Message from April Mitchell
Mar 9 – 6:49 PM
Me and the kids are hanging in
Loaded up on TP and hoping we don't catch it ha ha

Mar 9 – 7:15 PM
Stay safe girl were praying for you!!!

NY1 News @NY1 sent a Tweet
Mar 10 – 12:45 PM
216 cases of mysterious coronavirus now confirmed in New York
– ny1.co/459nyr

> Forwarded Tweet to Regina Schley
> Mar 10 – 8:46 PM
> Am I doing my math right or did we just get 195 new cases
> overnight?

You livestreamed Presidential WHO address https://youtu.be/
odalMjUNFqA
Mar 11 – 9:02 PM
9 min 28 sec   19K views

Text from Regina Schley
Mar 11 – 9:05 PM
Are you watching this?

Email from Jason Hines, Human Resources
<jason@tigerzoom.ai>
Mar 11 – 10:49 PM
Subject: WFH

Dear Fellow Tigers:

TigerZoom is closely monitoring health updates around the world in order to ensure our team's safety and well being. In light of the World Health Organization (WHO) declaring the novel coronavirus a global pandemic, leadership is making the below changes:

- All company travel is now suspended.
- Employees are requested to work from home the following two weeks effective immediately. If materials or equipment presently in the office are required to do your job, please contact your supervisor. He will arrange a time for you to securely retrieve those items.

- If you are experiencing coronavirus symptoms, you must notify HR ASAP. A list of symptoms is available on the CDC website here.

NY1 News @NY1 sent a Tweet
Mar 14 – 10:54 AM
NY sees 1st confirmed coronavirus-related death, 613 cases: ny1.co/461rfc

Direct Message from April Mitchell
Mar 16 – 7:08 PM
I cant believe they closed Saks thats my happy place

Direct Message to April Mitchell
Mar 16 – 7:09 PM
Yeah. My friend Michael works at the Lancome counter. They told everybody to file temporary unemployment for the next month.

Direct Message from April Mitchell
Mar 16 – 7:11 PM
Cool do you get free samples?

Text from Caroline Hampton
Mar 16 – 8:35 PM
Hey lady. Long time no text
Saw they're shutting stores and stuff up there in NYC. You need anything?

Missed call Momma
Mar 16 – 9:35 PM

NY1 News @NY1 sent a Tweet
Mar 16 – 10:08 PM
Coronavirus cases in New York now 1,000+, 12 New Yorkers dead
– ny1.co/398rkq

Regina Schley retweeted
New York Post @nypost Mar 17
As coronavirus spreads, New York's wealthy flee for Hamptons, safer climes.

Email from Milton Stults <miltonstults145@bellsouth.net>
Mar 17 – 7:45 AM
Subject: EMAIL FROM YOUR COUSIN MILT AND BARBARA

Hey cuz. Saw on the news where a lot of this virus stuff is going around New York city. You doing all right there? Love Cousin Milt and Barbara

Forwarded Tweet from April Mitchell
Mar 17 – 4:19 PM
NOOOOOOooooooooooooooooo

 Empire State Building ✓ @EmpireStateBldg · Mar 16
The Empire State Building closely monitors the development of COVID-19.
Preventive measures recommended by the CDC & NYC Department of
Health have been taken. The ESB Observatories are closed at this time.
Please check empirestatebuilding.com & our social channels for updates.

Missed call Faith Blanford
Mar 17 – 6:45 PM

NY1 News @NY1 sent a Tweet
Mar 17 – 9:19 PM
New York state coronavirus cases soar to approx 1,700 – ny1.co/346ytp

Email to Milton Stults
Mar 17 – 11:05 PM
Subject: re: EMAIL FROM YOUR COUSIN MILT AND BARBARA

Thanks, Milt. Appreciate you and Barbara checking in. I'm hunkered
down, as Aunt Emily would have said. Just got an email from work
that four people in my office have this now. I've been working from
home the last few days, though, so don't worry. I'm alright.

Text from Jenny Lindhauer
Mar 18 – 9:16 AM
Hey lady! So what's it like there?
Is it as bad as they say on the news?
#NewYorkStrong my friend!!

Direct Message from April Mitchell
Mar 18 – 11:32 AM

Wish we were doing this right now!! #saks #fifthavenue

Direct Message to April Mitchell
Mar 18 – 4:43 PM
That's sweet. Thanks. Hope you and the kids are well.

Text from Caroline Hampton
Mar 18 – 7:54 PM
Hey Maggie not sure you got my text a couple days ago
You still live in New York?

Missed call Robin Graham
Mar 18 – 8:02 PM

NY1 News @NY1 sent a Tweet
Mar 18 – 9:15 PM
As Testing Expands, Confirmed Cases of Coronavirus in N.Y.C.
Near 2,000.

Text from 270-885-4892
18 Mar – 9:17 PM
This still ur number
Worried about u being in NYC

Email from Milton Stults <miltonstults145@bellsouth.net>
19 Mar – 7:15 AM
Subject: WE NEED TO GET YOU OUT OF THERE!

Glad to hear you are staying at the house! Praying for you. If you
can refugee as far as the Ohio River, we can drive up and get you.
Unfortunately with Barbara's back, we can't really drive any further.

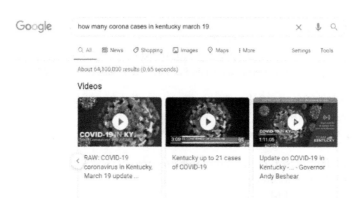

Email to Milton Stults
19 Mar – 11:59 PM
Subject: re: WE NEED TO GET YOU OUT OF THERE!

Hi, Milt. I don't really think it's safe to travel right now, but thank you. That's so sweet of y'all to ask. I wouldn't want to risk coming home, though, then giving it to all of you. From everything I've seen, Kentucky's cases are still low and it's not in anyone's best interest for me to become y'all's patient zero. 4 or 5 people from work have it now. I'm still working from home, though, so don't worry.

Love to you and Barbara.

Email from Milton Stults <miltonstults145@bellsouth.net>
20 Mar – 6:59 AM
Subject: Re: re: WE NEED TO GET YOU OUT OF THERE!

Let us know if you change your mind.

Text to Regina Schley
Mar 23 – 10:16 PM
Hey, have you been able to find bread? We're out on the UWS

Text from Regina Schley
Mar 23 – 10:18 PM
Yes, but there's no milk. You?

Email from Jason Hines, Human Resources
<jason@tigerzoom.ai>
Mar 23 – 10:52 PM
Subject: A Note from Our CEO

Dear Fellow Tigers:
TigerZoom has adapted far better than imagined to the economic pressures beginning to surface from this global pandemic. We're delivering at high efficiency and customer satisfaction rates remain high. As a technology-first company, it should be of no surprise to anyone that TigerZoom functions brilliantly in the cloud.

Many corporations have retracted their original financial projections due to the profound uncertainty in current consumer and business demand for products, goods, and services. Thanks to your efforts, we are weathering the storm with numbers well above projections. TigerZoom is on track for a highly profitable Q3!

This said, the global outlook remains difficult to forecast. To ensure TigerZoom remains competitive, effective this week all Tigers will experience a 10% salary reduction. We will also begin implementing mandatory overtime for marketing and sales personnel.

Now get out there and ROAR!
Jim Menley, CEO

April Mitchell sent a Tweet
Mar 24 – 4:23 PM
#whencoronaisover #prayersforNYC thinking of my friend
@KentuckianinNY #coronapocalyse #nycshutdown

April Mitchell pinned Tweet

Missed call Robin Graham
Mar 24 – 4:31 PM

Text from Faith Blanford
Mar 24 – 5:15 PM
Maggie you OK?

Missed call 270-885-4892
Mar 24 – 8:32 PM

Text to Regina Schley
Mar 24 – 8:33 PM
Are you getting a lot of texts from non-NY people?

Text from Regina Schley
Mar 24 – 8:35 PM
OH MY GOSH YES
You too?

Text to Regina Schley
Mar 24 – 8:36 PM
Gah! Like people I haven't spoken to in years
YEARS

Text from Regina Schley
Mar 24 – 8:39 PM
Tell me about it.
Yesterday this woman left me a three min voice mail about how upset she was that we're no longer in touch and how upset she is I might die. It was so long my iPhone actually cut her off mid sentence
Maggie, I kid you not. I had to fucking Google to see who she was. I was like how did this woman even get my number.

Text to Regina Schley
Mar 24 – 8:41 PM
You're shitting me

Text from Regina Schley
Mar 24 – 8:43 PM
Turns out she was my hairdresser when I lived in CA

Text to Regina Schley
Mar 24 – 8:44 PM
And I thought this girl from high school was bad

Text from Regina Schley
Mar 24 – 8:44 PM
???

Text to Regina Schley
Mar 24 – 8:45 PM
Go look at the Twitter feed for @TheRealAprilM
I think I sat next to her in algebra or something
I just follow her to be polite

Text from Regina Schley
Mar 24 – 8:57 PM
Are you fucking kidding me? *insert rolling eyes emoji here*
You're her best friiiiiiiiiiiend

Text to Regina Schley
Mar 24 – 9:15 PM
You know it. She's daming me all the time now
*DMing

Text from Regina Schley
Mar 24 – 9:15 PM
Fuck her. She just wants somewhere free to stay next time she's in the city. They all do

Missed call Momma
Mar 24 – 9:21 PM

Missed call Barbara
Mar 25 – 6:49 AM

Email from Milton Stults <miltonstults145@bellsouth.net>
Mar 25 – 7:05 AM
Subject: Fwd: Re: re:WE NEED TO GET YOU OUT OF THERE!

Barbara wants to know if you're good on toilet paper. She and Mellie raided the Dollar Store right when all this stuff hit. Want us to mail you a roll?

Email to Milton Stults
Mar 26 – 1:48 PM
Subject: Re: Fwd: Re: re: WE NEED TO GET YOU OUT OF THERE!

Thanks, Milt. That is so sweet. To be honest, what we need up here most right now is food. I managed to make it to the bodega yesterday (that's like our little corner store) and the guy there said the vendors they get their food from still have supplies, but the delivery people are refusing to drive into the city because they're afraid they'll get corona.

Mother offered to overnight me something with dry ice, but I'll be honest. The UPS people aren't running either and the mail routes are even crumbling. Route carriers aren't showing for work, their substitutes are no showing — service is sporadic and not everything's making it.

Last week, we had delivery Mon-Wed from our regular lady, then a sub came Thrs, then there was no mail Fri, Sat, or this Mon. They did come yesterday, but have not yet come today (and yes, the mail normally would have been here by now). Anything you send would be delayed, lost, or stolen. But I sure do appreciate your asking.

Email from Milton Stults <miltonstults145@bellsouth.net>
Mar 26 – 3:19 PM
Subject: Re: re: Fwd: Re: re: WE NEED TO GET YOU OUT OF THERE!

You remember that movie The Postman? Heh heh. Your Aunt Emily sure did love it.

Missed call Barbara
Mar 30 – 6:04 PM

Missed call Aunt Jodi
Mar 30 – 6:05 PM

Text from 270-885-4892

Mar 30 – 6:06 PM
OMG REFRIGERATION TRUCKS??!

Missed call Momma
Mar 30 – 6:06 PM

Text from 270-885-4892
Mar 30 – 6:07 PM
Can u see them?1?1?!

Text from Faith Blanford
Mar 30 – 6:09 PM
**Are they really putting people inside refrigerators up there that's what
Bobby said they said on the news but i don't believe it call us!**

Text from Momma
Mar 30 – 6:11 PM
**Sweetheart, please call me. Your daddy just saw on the news where
they're having to put those poor people's bodies into freezer trucks. Are
you okay?**

Email from Milton Stults <miltonstults145@bellsouth.net>
Mar 30 – 6:13 PM
Subject: Fwd: Re: re: Fwd: Re: re: WE NEED TO GET YOU OUT OF
THERE!

SURE YOU DON'T WANT TO COME HOME? BARBARA AND I CAN
DRIVE AS FAR AS CINCINNATI TO GET YOU.

Text to Regina Schley
Mar 30 – 6:14 PM
Have you heard about this refrigeration truck thing?

Text from Regina Schley
Mar 30 – 6:15 PM
YES. It's all over the news

Google it

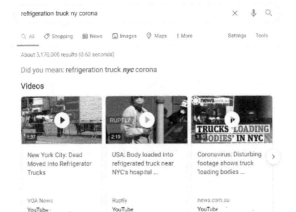

Missed call Momma
Mar 30 – 6:17 PM

Text to Momma
Mar 30 – 6:18 PM

Momma, I'm fine. Please don't worry.

Could you maybe ask people to stop calling and texting so much? That
would really help me out.

I'm still trying to work over here.

Mar 30 – 6:25 PM

Maybe if people back home want to know how I'm doing, they could get
information from you?

Like centralize it somehow? Maybe set up an information chain?

Email from Milton Stults <miltonstults145@bellsouth.net>
Mar 30 – 6:39 PM
Subject: Fwd: Fwd: Re: re: Fwd: Re: re: WE NEED TO GET YOU
OUT OF THERE!

Hey cuz. Your mother told us you don't really want people calling
you right now because you're overwhelmed. You can always move
back home to good ole Kentuck!

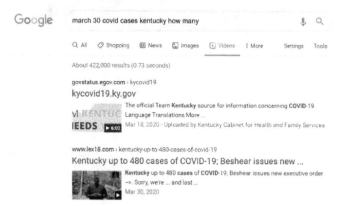

You now follow WKDZ Radio @WKDZ
Breaking news, sports, and weather for the Western Kentucky
region
Cadiz, Ky   Joined Twitter May 2009

Text from 270-885-4892
Mar 30 – 8:43 PM
Looking pretty bad up there u thought about moving home

Regina Schley retweeted
CBS New York @CBSNY Mar 31
US Navy Ship Comfort arrives in New York City; US death toll tops 3,100

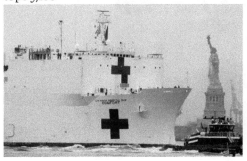

You now follow CBS New York @CBSNY
Your source for NY news, weather, sports & traffic streaming 24/7.
New York, NY   Joined Twitter September 2008

You now follow NBC New York @NBCNewYork
Breaking news and StormTeam 4 weather updates. Stories from New York's biggest investigative unit.
New York, NY   Joined Twitter August 2008

You now follow New York Daily News @NYDailyNews
NYC's Original Hometown Paper 🍎 National news with a NY lens, covering sports & entertainment for all 5 boroughs
New York City   Joined Twitter October 2007

You now follow PIX11 News @PIX11News
New York's hometown station since 1948. Every story hits home.
New York, NY   Joined Twitter October 2007

CBS New York @CBSNY sent a Tweet
Mar 31 – 10:27 PM
NYC Death Toll Passes 1000 as Mayor Pleads for Help

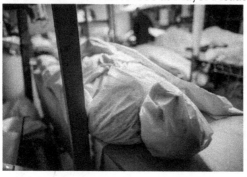

Text to Regina Schley
Apr 1 – 7:19 PM
Michael got attacked at the laundry mat yesterday

Text from Regina Schley
Apr 1 – 7:23 PM
WTF he left his apartment?

Text to Regina Schley
Apr 1 – 7:26 PM
Yeah I just got off the phone with him
**He was trying to take his stuff out of the dryer and this crazy lady ran up
and just grabbed him by the shoulders and started shaking and hitting
him yelling, "You're not distancing you're not distancing"**

Text from Regina Schley
Apr 1 – 7:28 PM
Oh my G-d. I am SO glad I have laundry in my building

Text to Regina Schley
Apr 1 – 7:28 PM
I wish I did

Text from Regina Schley
Apr 1 – 7:29 PM
Oh right
So are you not going outside at all?

Text to Regina Schley
Apr 1 – 7:30 PM
Outside? 😜 What's that?

Text from Regina Schley
Apr 1 – 7:30 AM
Nice

Apr 1 – 7:32 AM
So what are you doing for underwear?

Text to Regina Schley
Apr 1 – 7:33 PM
Wearing them inside out

Text from Regina Schley
Apr 1 – 7:33 PM
(typing ellipsis)
...
(deleting ellipsis)

Direct Message from April Mitchell
Apr 1 – 9:45 PM
Did you hear Coronas over!

Apr 1 – 9:46 PM
APRIL FOOLS!!!!

Regina Schley retweeted
Eyewitness News @ABC7NY Apr 1
N.Y.C. Virus Death Toll Approaches 1,400

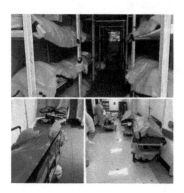

You now follow Eyewitness News @ABC7NY
New York's #1 News, Channel 7 Eyewitness News, WABC-TV –
Download app to livestream.
New York City   Joined Twitter October 2008

Text from Regina Schley
Apr 3 – 2:14 PM
MILK AT D'AGOSTINO!
GO GO GO

April Mitchell mentioned you in a Tweet
Apr 3 – 4:45 PM
RT if you have a friend in NYC #NYCstrong @KentuckianinNY
love you girl! #staysafe #corona #coronavirusNYC

Text from Regina Schley
Apr 3 – 11:45 PM
So I'm totally following that weird April girl on Twitter now
Is that picture from your high school yearbook?!?!!!!!!!!

Apr 3 – 11:48 PM
BTW Did you get milk?

New York Daily News @NYDailyNews sent a Tweet
Apr 3 – 11:53 PM
N.Y. Virus Deaths Double in Three Days to Almost 3,000

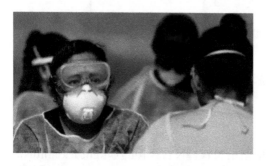

You have unfollowed @NYDailyNews

Text to Momma
Apr 4 – 7:16 AM

Text from Momma
Apr 4 – 7:19 AM
Hi, sweetheart. Did you mean to send me a picture of a helicopter?

Text to Momma
Apr 4 – 7:23 AM
Whoops. That was for Regina.

Text to Regina Schley
Apr 4 – 7:23 AM

Text from Momma
Apr 4 – 7:24 AM
Oh. Sorry.

Text from Regina Schley
Apr 4 – 7:25 AM
Oh my G-d yes. Make them stop

Text from Momma
Apr 4 – 7:25 AM
So what's the story with the helicopter? ☺
Your daddy and I are learning how to use emojis. ☺☺☺

Text to Momma
Apr 4 – 7:26 AM

Sorry. They've been circling my place a couple days now.
They start up at about 7 in the morning and go until 10 or 11 at night.
It's getting old

Missed call Momma
Apr 4 – 7:27 AM

Text from Momma
Apr 4 – 7:28 AM

Sorry I missed you. Why are there helicopters?
Your daddy wants to know if we send you a care package, will you get
it. Has the mail gone back to running?

Text to Momma
Apr 4 – 7:29 AM

(typing ellipsis)

...

(deleting ellipsis)

They're carrying dead bodies from the field hospital in Central Park to
the Navy ship on the Hudson. I live under the flight path.

Missed call Momma
Apr 4 – 7:31 AM

Missed call Momma
Apr 4 – 7:32 AM

Text to Momma
Apr 4 – 7:36 AM

I'm working Momma sorry

Oh, honey.
You don't know that they're dead. Maybe it's supplies.
Or maybe they're carrying sick people to the Navy hospital to get them
help?

(typing ellipsis)

...

(deleting ellipsis)

Email from Jason Hines, Human Resources
<jason@tigerzoom.ai>
Apr 4 – 1:42 PM
Subject: A Note from Our CEO Dear Fellow Tigers:

TigerZoom is not immune to the emotional health concerns many of
our Tigers are facing. As a people-first company, it's important to us
that you have access to the very best resources to help us roar
through this together. That's why we've signed up each and every
one of you for virtual yoga classes, accessible by clicking here. And
since overtime is now mandatory for all Tigers, we've worked hard
to ensure these classes are available to you 24-7.

If you are experiencing suicidal thoughts, please notify HR ASAP.

Now get out there and ROAR!
Jim Menley, CEO

PIX11 News @PIX11News sent a Tweet
Apr 4 – 12:23 PM
With 2,624 fatalities in New York City alone, governor says: "It is like a fire spreading."

Text from Regina Schley
Apr 5 – 1:43 PM
A tiger has this now. A fucking tiger.
https://newyork.cbslocal.com/2020/04/05/coronavirus-bronx-zoo-tiger-tests-positive/

Direct Message from April Mitchell
Apr 5 – 4:43 PM
Maggie are you okay? Haven't heard from you in a while!!
DM ME!!!!

April Mitchell mentioned you in a Tweet
Apr 5 – 5:15 PM
SOOoooo worried about my friend @KentuckianinNY she lives
in Manhattan. Haven't heard from her in DAAAAYS ☹ ☹ ☹

Text from Regina Schley
Apr 6 – 12:39 AM
What the genuine fuck is wrong with that girl?

Apr 6 – 12:40 AM
Have you been on Twitter? Check out weird April's feed

Text to Regina Schley
Apr 6 – 8:14 AM
Oh I know

Text from Regina Schley
Apr 6 – 2:18 PM
BLOCK HER

Text to Regina Schley
Apr 6 – 3:01 PM
I hate my job I hate my job I hate my job

Apr 6 – 3:04 PM
15 hours yesterday

Text from Regina Schley
Apr 6 – 3:09 PM
Tell them they can't pay you less and expect more work

Text to Regina Schley
Apr 6 – 4:03 PM
It's not just me it's everybody
The woman I share an office with only got three hours sleep last night

Text from Regina Schley
Apr 6 – 4:04 PM
Oh whose getting any sleep these dats?
*days

Text to Regina Schley
Apr 6 – 4:06 PM
You don't get it. This morning they laid off 120 people
Everybody's too afarid to say no
Gotta go sorry

Apr 6 – 5:21 PM
Hang in there okay?

Email from Milton Stults <miltonstults145@bellsouth.net>
Apr 6 – 6:45 PM
Subject: Fwd: Fwd: Fwd: Re: re: Fwd: Re: re: WE NEED TO GET
YOU OUT OF THERE!

Hey cuz. Haven't heard from you in a couple days. Let me and
Barbara know you're okay.

Text to Momma
Apr 6 – 8:13 PM
Momma, can you let Milt know I'm not dead?

Text from Unknown
Apr 6 – 10:18 PM

Are you quarantined and horney? Mask wearing hotttties video sex hxjk.co

Report SPAM to 7726
Apr 6 – 10:19 PM

Forwarded Tweet from Regina Schley
Apr 6 – 11:16 PM

Neil Webb
@neilmwebb

"You are not working from home; you are at your home during a crisis trying to work."

I've heard this twice today. I think it's an important distinction worth emphasising.

5:39 PM · Mar 31, 2020 · Twitter Web App

77.4K Retweets   **280.8K** Likes

EMERGENCY ALERT
Apr 6 – 11:43 PM

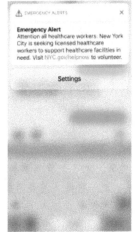

Text to Regina Schley
Apr 6 – 11:45 PM
Did you get this?

Text from Regina Schley
Apr 6 – 11:47 PM
We're all gonna die

Regina Schley retweeted
New York Post @nypost Apr 6
72,181 confirmed cases, at least 2,475 New Yorkers dead.

You now follow New York Post @nypost
Features & breaking news from The New York Post. @pagesix,
@nypmetro, @nypostbiz, @nypostsports, @nypfashion,
@nypostopinion
New York, NY   Joined Twitter November 2008

Missed call Momma
Apr 7 – 9:05 AM

Text from Momma
Apr 7 – 9:06 AM

Honey, call when you get a moment, please. There's nothing wrong.
Your daddy and I just miss you. Love you, sweetheart.

NY1 News @NY1 sent a Tweet
Apr 7 – 12:45 PM
NYC now accounts for 25% of all novel coronavirus deaths in
the US. When will the city reach its peak? pix11.com/
livecoronaupdates

Text from Momma

Apr 7 – 1:34 PM

You're not going outside any, are you? Try to get some exercise

somehow.

PIX11 retweeted
Elena Torres PIX11 @PIX11Elena Apr 7
Longest line yet #TraderJoeHarlem stretches from 6th to 8th
Aves after other area grocery stores close. More at 11. #COVID19
#coronapocolypse #foodshortage #runningout

April Mitchell mentioned you in a Tweet
Apr 7 – 4:19 PM
You bring the corona @KentuckianinNY I'll bring the lime

You know what goes great
with the Corona virus?

Lyme Disease

Regina Schley retweeted
New York Post @nypost Apr 8
Still not enough ventilators, doctors say, with one New Yorker
dead every minute

Text from Momma
Apr 8 – 5:48 PM
Honey, are you okay?
Your daddy and I love you, sweetheart, very much.

Google   how to rent a car during corona   ✕   🎤   🔍

🔍 All   📰 News   ▶ Videos   🖼 Images   🛍 Shopping   ⋮ More   Settings   Tools

About 1,800,000,000 results (0.55 seconds)

www.enterprise.com › car-rental › on-call-for-all › covi... ▾
Enterprise COVID-19 (Coronavirus) FAQs | Enterprise Rent-A ...
Can I rent a car at the airport during the Coronavirus outbreak? Yes, our airport locations are
open. Find an airport car rental location and start a reservation.

www.businessinsider.com › ... › Travel › Transportation ▾
Experts reveal whether rental cars are safe to drive right now ...
Jump to What should I know about a rental car's cleaning policies for ... But while the pandemic
continues, and with a vaccine for Covid-19 ...

www.nymetroparents.com › article › renting-a-car-duri... ▾
Renting a Car During Coronavirus | NYMetroParents
Can you safely rent a car during coronavirus? What precautions are car rental
companies taking to limit spread?

www.autoslash.com › blog-and-tips › posts › coronavir... ▾
Car Rentals During Coronavirus Pandemic | AutoSlash
May 29, 2020 · Do you need a rental car in the coming weeks or months? Here's what to know
about renting a car amid the coronavirus pandemic.

WKDZ Radio @WKDZ sent a Tweet
Apr 8 – 6:43 PM
Governor's request that Kentuckians wear masks in public
sparks controversy

Text to Momma
Apr 8 – 6:44 PM

I know all y'all want me to come home but I'm going to wait it out up
here, Momma, sorry.

Regina Schley retweeted
New York Times @nytimes Apr 9
Grueling workloads, unprecedented stress result in health care
worker suicides across city – nyt.co/fj87k5

April Mitchell @TheRealAprilM sent a Tweet
Apr 9 – 4:16 PM
Thank GOD for our essential workers! Love my hard working
cousin @real_sally_b @medicalcenterBG#curethechinavirus
#gotomyetsyforPPE #dancingnurses

Tagged in this photo: @KentuckianinNY

Text to Regina Schley
Apr 10 – 8:35 PM
Hey, do you know how to untag yourself from a photo on Twitter?

You have nine missed calls.

You livestreamed New York Governor Daily Briefing
https://youtu.be/wtfHNFqL
Apr 11 – 12:01 PM
41 min 57 sec 309K views

Outbound call Regina Schley
Apr 12 – 1:26 PM

Text to Regina Schley
Apr 12 – 1:27 PM
REGINA CALL ME BACK
Please call me back I just saw a woman try to throw herself off the
balcony across the street oh my god oh my God she just went out there
and started screaming and yelling and beating her chest with her fists
like some sort of animal and I just happen to be looking out the window
and saw her my God I don't know what to do she just started renching
her clothes like they do in the Bible and then she just reached out and
grabbed the fire escape and started shaking it and tried to throw herself
over and I've never seen anything like that in my life oh my God Regina
call me back

Outbound call 911
Apr 12 – 1:28 PM

April Mitchell sent a Tweet
Apr 12 – 4:43 PM
Still haven't heard from my friend!#PrayersforNYC
#prayformyfriendmaggie

You livestreamed New York Governor Daily Briefing
https://youtu.be/wthWFDfT Apr 13 – 12:16 PM
50 min 37 sec 662K views

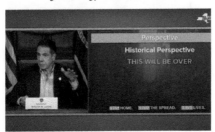

Text from Regina Schley
Apr 23 – 11:56 PM
I can not watch anymore television No mas no mas no mas
Can. NOt.
no

Apr 23 – 11:58 PM
did you ever realzie how many alien epidemics they get on Star Trek the
nex generationn
?

Apr 24 – 12:03 AM
i think every bad episode of Star Trek is because de Anna Troy made a
more life desciion
poor life decision
fuck spell auto correct

Apr 24 – 12:10 AM
Maggie, helllloooooooooo
You up?

Apr 24 – 1:02 PM
So hungover Sorry

Regina Schley retweeted
New York Times @nytimes Apr 29
NYPD arrest funeral home director for filling U-Haul trucks with

dozens of bodies, director says "There's no space."

Missed call Aunt Jodi Cell
Apr 29 – 6:13 PM

Missed call Aunt Jodi and Uncle Reuben Home
Apr 29 – 6:15 PM

Text from Aunt Jodi
Apr 29 – 6:16 PM
Hi Maggie it's Aunt Jodi
Not sure if you get texts
Your Uncle Reuben has the news on
He said they just said the funeral homes have run out of room and their
putting people into U-Haul
Is that correct
Please call us

Apr 29 – 6:21 PM
Maggie did you get my text its Aunt Jodi
We think you should come home now
Please call

Text to Momma
Apr 29 – 6:21 PM
Please tell Aunt Jodi I'm alive

Text from Momma
Apr 29 – 6:22 PM
She just called the house.
Are you still working?

Text to Momma
Apr 29 – 6:29 PM
I'm always working. She's annoying the shit out of me
Seriously can these people not centralize information?
Sorry I said shit

You have 1 new voice mail from Mount Sinai Hospital
Apr 29 – 10:49 PM

Text to Momma
Apr 29 – 11:48 PM
Momma, I don't know if I can do this anymore
Momma I wanna come home

Apr 29 – 11:49 PM
I wanna come home, Momma
We're dying everywhere. Tell everyone we're dying everywhere

Missed call Momma
Apr 30 – 6:45 AM

Missed call Momma
Apr 30 – 7:15 AM

Text from Momma
Apr 30 – 8:03 AM
Sweetheart, we will come get you. Your daddy and I are happy to come
get you. I don't know how we'll do it. We can quarantine you in our
room because of the half-bath.

Apr 30 – 8:04 AM
Sweetheart, are you awake?

Missed call Momma
Apr 30 – 8:07 AM

Text from Momma
Apr 30 – 8:15 AM
Okay, honey. Just let me know when you're up.
Your daddy and I love you.
🖤🖤🖤 😊😊😊

Apr 30 – 8:21 AM
Sweetheart, are you okay?

Text to Momma
Apr 30 – 9:49 AM
Sorry, Momma. Overslept
Y'all don't need to come get me
I need to work now

Apr 30 – 9:55 AM
Love you

Voice mail from Momma
Apr 30 – 10:06 AM

Text to Momma
Apr 30 – 11:04 AM
**I mean it. DO NOT COME UP HERE. Y'all don't need to be anywhere
near this
DO NOT COME PLEASE**

Apr 30 – 11:06 AM
Regina died last night is all

Missed call Momma
Apr 30 – 11:06 AM

Missed call Momma
Apr 30 – 11:10 AM

Missed call Momma
Apr 30 – 11:11 AM

Missed call Momma
Apr 30 – 11:12 AM

Email from Milton Stults <miltonstults145@bellsouth.net>
Apr 30 – 11:49 AM
Subject: MASK CARD BARBARA FOUND ON FACEBOOK

Hey cuz. Barbara and I saw on the news that they're making all y'all
wear face masks up there now so we found this online for you.
Barbara says print it out and you can carry it in stores with you and
then they can't make you put one on.

I am exempt from the Governor's
regulation mandating face mask usage
in public. Wearing a facemask poses a
health risk to me.

Under the ADA and HIPAA, I am not required
to disclose my medical conditions to you.

You sent a Tweet
Apr 30 – 12:13 PM

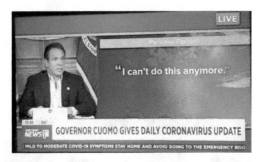

Email from Jason Hines, Human Resources via DocuSign
<dse_NA19@docusign.net>
May 1 – 12:41 AM
Subject: Employee Termination Agreement

Jason Hines has sent a document for you to review and sign.
REVIEW DOCUMENT HERE
Click to download the DocuSign app.

Text from Momma
May 1 – 8:15 AM
I love you, sweetheart.

New York Times @nytimes sent a Tweet
July 11 – 12:15 PM
NY's first day with no coronavirus deaths rfally arrives 132 days after the city's first case. White House health advisor points to Tenn, Ky outbreaks, cautions leaders: "We can't afford another surge."

Email from Milton Stults <miltonstults145@bellsouth.net>
July 14 – 7:43 AM
To: Barbara Stults, Margaret Brown, Aunt Marie, Aunt Jodi, Uncle Reuben, ghblanford942@gmail.com, dan3@bellsouth.net, Big George
Subject: Fwd: Fwd: fwd: Fwd: fwd: Ha ha funny

Begin forwarded message

You retweeted
WKDZ Radio @WKDZ July 21
Ky Gov. announces 613 new coronavirus cases, 2 deaths today,
single highest increase since March

April Mitchell replied to your Tweet
July 21 – 5:15 PM
@KentuckianinNY I see #MSM intentionally left out the fact
that hes closing restaurants down
#MakeKentuckyGreatAgain #letuswork

You replied to April Mitchell's Tweet
July 21 – 5:17 PM
@TheRealAprilM Seating at 25% capacity INDOORS isn't exactly what I'd call "closed down." We STILL aren't allowed to eat inside here at all. Plus y'all can always go to restaurants and sit outside.

April Mitchell replied to your Tweet
July 21 – 5:18 PM
@KentuckianinNY tell that to the waitress who just lost her job!! #impeachkygov #reopenky

You replied to April Mitchell's Tweet
July 21 – 5:18 PM
@TheRealAprilM Better unemployed than dead.

April Mitchell replied to your Tweet
July 21 – 5:19 PM
@KentuckianinNY and how many people will die of starvation cause they can't work during lockdown?!!

You replied to April Mitchell's Tweet
July 21 – 5:19 PM
@TheRealAprilM Remember you're talking to someone who lives in NY. You don't even know what a lockdown is. Ky is nowhere near that. All Kentuckians have ever been asked to do is #wearamask, stay 6 ft apart & get your chicken wings to go. That is not a lockdown.

April Mitchell replied to your Tweet
July 21 – 5:20 PM
@KentuckianinNY NOT TRUE you don't even live here anymore. Spas n schools are closed. You have no idea how hard our lockdown has been. It's not like you lost YOUR job! Quit acting like your special!!!! #reopenkynow

April Mitchell retweeted
Breitbart News @BreitbartNews July 21
Coronavirus far less deadly than claimed, Dems intentionally
manipulating data

You replied to April Mitchell's Tweet
July 21 – 5:21 PM
@TheRealAprilM My friend is dead. Helicopters flew dead
bodies over my apt EVERY DAY. We were told not to open our
WINDOWS up here. This is not a conspiracy. #wearadamnmask
#covIDIOT

April Mitchell replied to your Tweet
July 21 – 5:22 PM
@KentuckianinNY

You replied to April Mitchell's Tweet
July 21 – 5:22 PM
@TheRealAprilM Despite your many ill-informed & poorly
worded memes, corona is no laughing matter. Yeah, I live in NY
now, but all that means is I know what I'm talking about.
I've seen what this can do. You all need to stop being such
#covidiots #stayathome #stopthespread #wearamask

@TheRealAprilM blocked you

Text from Caroline Hampton
July 21 – 5:56 PM
I saw that tweet you sent April
How dare you go offon her like that
It's not like NYC was the only ones facing corona what makes you so
special

Text from Robin Graham
July 21 – 6:14 PM
You know I did my best to check on you and not once did you bother to
call me back
How dare you call April stupid
I hope you like it up there

Text from Jenny Lindhauer
July 21 – 6:17 PM
Have to admit, Maggie, low blow calling April an idiot on Twitter

Text from 270-885-4892
July 21 – 6:20 PM
Ur not dead it's not like u went through anything special
Stop telling us what to do
Why should we listen to u

NEW YORK

MARCH 2020

טיט
MORIMOS
আমরা
মারা যাচ্ছি
TUNAKUFA

WE ARE

МЫ УМИРАЕМ
אנחנו גוססים

DYI

NOUS
WIR STER BEN
NG
SOMMES
UMÍRÁME
EN TRAIN
ZOMIERAME
DE MOURIR

SOTI TUNAKUFA

НИЕ УМИРЕМО
УМИ
NOS ESTAN
PAME
VIENDO MORIR
ငါတို့သေကြပြီ
사망
ĐANG
MORREMOS
CHẾT
ME OLEMME
MAMATAY TAYO
KUOLEMASSA
我们快死了

YOU ARE

WATCHING
US DIE

REGRESSION

_____

I. Alzheimer's Disease: Preclinical

I'm not mad; I'm angry. I've done everything right: learned
something new every day, eaten my leafy greens. I don't care if
my mother had it — or so the doctors said — her mother before
her and my aunt. There was a chance. As long as I was young,
there was still a chance. I could believe. But there's no doubting
it now. They say I won't lose my memories, just my ability to
retrieve them. And what good'll that do, a life under lock and
chains? Everything I am — or everything I was — my sense of
self, my identity — trapped, rattling away in here?

II. Mild Cognitive Impairment

I'm   mad.   Angry. I've done everything right: learned
something   every day, eaten my   greens. I don't care if
     mother had it — or   the doctors said   her mother before
her?   There was a chance.   I was young,
          still   . I could believe.   There's no doubt
   now!   I won't lose my memories-just my
                                        life,
          everything I am — or everything I was — my
self   identity — trapped   away in here.

III. Moderate Decline

I'm   angry. I   do   everything right: learn
something   every day, eat   my   greens,
     Mother   said.
                                             I was young
          still   , I   believe.
     Now   my memories,
                                          life,
          everything's
                         trapped   in here.

IV. Late-Stage

I   do   everything,

     Mother   said.
                                             I was young
          still   , I   believe.
     Now.
                                          life
                    's
                                     in here.

V. Fully Progressed

I

     m

          still

                                    here.

74

23,195 NEW YORKERS AND COUNTING

The people next door are gone — gone as in left the city, not dead — though it takes a couple months for me to know it, my friend Emaline asking — over the phone, of course — what time I'm waking up these days. A couple weeks in, maybe week number two, week number three, I tell her, I just said screw it and decided to turn off the alarm.

So you get up when you get up, she said and I answered, Yeah.

We are on the long stretch home of month number three when I realize I don't hear anything next door anymore, that the reason I'm sometimes able to sleep as late as 8, 8:30, 9 isn't that my alarm's turned off, but theirs, the only sound through the wall that connected us, iPhone resonance exactly ten minutes before mine. I haven't heard it for quite some time, I think, and that's when I know they are gone.

Our building was one of the ones that emptied early, pseudo-rich west-siders making their way toward safer climes: Pennsylvania, the Hamptons, Connecticut. I could have gone too but I didn't, worried I'd infect my family back home. Take a walk, my mother says not thinking, then shakes her head over FaceTime, Don't.

In other parts of the country, life is different, but not completely changed, people still able to roam about, drive by friends' houses and wave from their cars. I don't tell them about the helicopters, the ones lifting dead bodies from the field hospital in Central

Park. You can hear birds, I say, fifteen years living in New York and finally I hear birds.

At 7 o'clock, there is the banging. It's supposed to mean we're grateful, the city's symbol it's alive, and in the beginning, Emaline says it gave her hope. What can you see, she asks, explaining all she can see is a wall, that tiny bit of a wall from the building across the street, afraid to open her window, to lean out. I'm not about to catch this, she tells me. When all this is over, you and I, we're going to yoga.

Emaline and I have never gone to yoga together, not even once, largely because she hates all sorts of exercise. I for one go to Bryant Park. Every Thursday, they hold free classes — or at least they did — and if you look down on them from the Grace Building, you can see how minuscule we are. The mats become pink dots, bodies folding in a row, and you think how small we are, how small we are and the office I worked in is only on the fifteenth floor.

The virus, they tell us, is one fourth of the size of the holes in any mask that's built to protect you — even the elusive N95, hard and tight and hotter in the city right now than a Magnolia cupcake — small enough to drive a Mack truck through those stupid bandanas they sell online.

What sort of person thinks a piece of fabric could protect them, that's what I want to know, Emaline says, sharing the story of her friend Ellen who went outside: Ellen went to the grocery and this man behind her in line wouldn't distance, was standing right behind her like he would have before — as close as though it were any old line — and Ellen started crying, caught between him and the cashier, the cashier telling the man to back away, while he said, it's okay, you don't have to distance if you wear a mask, every syllable, every sound, a droplet dagger that could kill her.

What an imbecile, Emaline said. I mean, you don't rear end somebody just because they have a bumper on their car. If people did what they were supposed to and simply stayed away from each other, all of this would be over.

People hate to be alone, I tell her, week six or week five, then four days after the grocery incident Emaline says Ellen got sick. Bet that man feels pretty good right now. Wonder how many people he infected with his asymptomatic self.

And that's the thing. This disease is silent, quieter than the city has to be to hear birds. No one knows they have it until they pass out or begin coughing like mad, so many in the hospitals sick, filling the halls, a freezer truck for their bodies. It's the herpes of non-STD's, we laugh, you know, that guy who won't use a condom because he swears he doesn't have it when 90 percent of people never get a wart.

I don't think you get warts with that, I say, they're sores, then See, there you go, Emaline answers, Nobody knows what any of this stuff ever looks like.

That night I stare at my vagina too long in the tub, Googling images of herpes, folliculitis, HPV. It's unhealthy, preternatural to spend so much time submerged, looking at one's parts, and I sit there so long the 7 o'clock banging, it comes and it goes, yet still I stay in the water. I'll get up when I get up, I think, then wonder who else is gone.

PRIVACY STATION

At night, as Emma lay sleeping, Aaron would look at her. He'd walk into her room and kneel beside her, bend down to the same level as the bed and watch her face. She was unchanged. During the day, he could see it, the difference the years had made: small wrinkles now formed between her eyebrows, soft lines across her forehead when she concentrated on a task.

Just that morning, he'd watched as Emma had grafted a tree, slicing clean into the branch, bandaging it back with white ribbon. He'd walked up to place his hand under hers, to help give the limb more support, then he saw it: a sunspot. The tiniest little mole between her trapezoid and trapezium knuckles, a dash.

What're you grinning at, she said and he answered, Nothing.

There were other signs of aging as well, things Aaron didn't think he would have caught if he'd been with Emma for always, if they hadn't spent all those years apart, things like a curly gray hair on the back of her head, visible only when she tied it up in a knot. Next time we decide to go into outer space, Emma told him, remind me to bring more ponytail holders.

You think they'll let you come twice, he said.

You did.

Then she moved in to kiss his cheek, and Aaron thought, No, Emma hasn't changed at all.

EARLY LOW BLUEBERRY

First to bloom is the early dwarf blueberry, the smallest of the whortleberry shrubs
we brought with us and the first to yield fruit. Due to their small size and
proximity to the ground, they were scarcely noticed on Earth prior to the Great
Berry Deadening of 2146. Here on station, we find them rather tasty.

They called it Privacy Station, they being Emma and Aaron. I'm not quite sure where the name comes from, he told her when she asked, I just found it scratched on the back of the bathroom door my first tour, making Emma realize right away this wasn't a name used on Earth. She'd never heard it during training, hadn't seen it in any of the materials. It certainly wasn't the name of the show, the 24-hour channel people back home could watch, giving orbiting scientists' families a way to keep tabs from the surface.

There is the bathroom, Emma said, there aren't any cameras in there. But there was one outside the door and they both wore a vestcam, its small light blinking off whenever they went inside. Not to mention Aaron was certain the producers had hidden more. Undisclosed cameras weren't supposed to be on (they explicitly went against contract) but Aaron didn't trust them, telling Emma that not even the bathroom was completely safe, that sometimes he thought the vestcams stayed on unless you were going number two, that he wouldn't be surprised if they weren't somehow still recording just in case (say, for example, she went in the bathroom and had a breakdown).

I'm just saying you're never alone, placing his palm upon the counter, spreading his fingers wide. You can't drop your guard. Then, speaking lower, With it just being us up here, that might get hard, especially because, well, since there is already a comfort level. Just remember they're watching, reaching out his hand to circle her wrist, don't forget, releasing.

It was the first time they'd touched since college, Aaron having accidentally brushed her arm only once back then, the exact same goosebumps rising. (In the late twentieth century, scientists had discovered each and every hair on the dionaea muscipula had memory, tendrils touched in the dark recalling the experience in light. And when Emma had stepped through the tunnel, the tunnel connecting her shuttle to the station, light was all there had been. Had she recognized him?

For a moment, Aaron had stood trapped. Was it better to say her name, letting everyone watching back home know that they had met? Or should he act like a stranger, keep that one small memory of longing to himself?)

Any moment you can get, Aaron told her, any taste of privacy at all, sliding his hand away, eyes flicking up to the camera, take it.

FLOWERING RASPBERRY

I, of course, came on station with hope. Who wouldn't in my position? We'd grown these on the farm back home; they're what I miss the most. Like others of their genus, the fruit itself is red, but what makes rubus odoratus different is its size. The berry itself is exceptionally large, but the individual plants never yielded very many.

Aaron was the better botanist between them and they both knew it. Emma's work was redemptive (after graduation, she'd focused more on the preservation of trees, Aaron on berries). A few years ago, she'd saved the maple, a non-fruit bearing tree, but one essential to the wildlife ecosystem. It was nothing that would win her awards, things like the Nobel and the Goldman going to projects that addressed the human food crisis. Emma had tried arguing that people ate squirrels and deer, animals that lived off of sugar maple bark, but no dice. Aaron, on the other hand, had won multiple awards, constantly presenting at this conference or that, Emma seeing his name in journals respected planetwide. He hadn't won a Nobel yet, but still.

Aaron succeeding, she was glad to see. The fact that he was

married, she was not, Emma periodically searching his name after college with the word "divorced?"

It wasn't like she'd thought about him for years. In fact, she'd actually stopped thinking about him way too early. Aaron had been a senior Emma's freshman year and even when they both were enrolled, they barely spent any time together. There'd been department mixers, sure, but Emma was friends more with the astrophysics and computer science majors, went to fraternity parties and technoclubs. Meanwhile Aaron, he stuck to his plants, spending Friday and Saturday nights monitoring the passages that help air flow down to roots. In college (just as now), the scientific community wasn't sure why the berries had all disappeared. Being scientists, they thought they knew, developing theory after theory then debunked. So Aaron, he decided early to examine the growth of a plant from the proverbial ground up. I'm not saying I'll stop world hunger, he'd told her, Emma running into him one night in the basement botany lab. But the more I learn about how berries grow period, all of it from root to flora, the better I can help.

This single conversation wasn't enough to make Emma fall in love, but it was enough to make her think there might be something, something to Aaron other women overlooked. It wasn't what he said so much as the way he'd reached out his hand when he said it, accidentally brushing her arm, honesty in words and gaze. So the next morning, she called their friend Sean and said, Well, me and Aaron, how 'bout it?

When Emma saw Aaron had been selected for Privacy Station (the first time he'd gone, not now, watching his year on the show from home), she was elated. Finally, she thought, somebody qualified.

FLOWERING RASPBERRY

Fossils show that in the century pre-Deadening, the rubus odoratus did not experience much evolution. This comes as no surprise since periods of consistent environmental conditions favor the status quo. When conditions change, however, the plants that are able to mutate most quickly are the ones that survive. Accordingly, one might theorize that in the most difficult of habitats, new development would happen most quickly. Yet in space, we find it's subtle environmental shifts that push new fruit to grow. Like people, plants must evolve or become static (ie, recede into extinction). With the Deadening, an as-yet-unknown factor either pushed every berry into that static state or suddenly overwhelmed even the most adaptable of plants. It is my hope that under these smaller, environmental changes in space that the flowering raspberry will once again yield harvest. Today, I germinated what few seeds I had remaining from the farm, placing each one in a different environment. Fingers crossed.

The first three weeks they were on board, Aaron felt he could do nothing. The longer people stayed on Privacy Station, the harder it became for them to not get used to the cameras, to not become complacent. Most scientists, over time, conveniently forgot the world was watching. It was the only way, the producers had told him, that orbiters could grow comfortable enough to continue with their work, go on with some semblance of daily life. And Aaron's first tour, it had taken a couple months (maybe two, maybe three) to keep the nervousness of it all from impacting his research, constantly scrutinizing every notation in his head, jotting down figures just to cross them out then write them down again. There wasn't just the sense that another scholar might be watching and disagree; this, he'd grown used to quickly enough (having spent his adult life conducting research in labs with security cameras and the like). It was everything else. What part of Aaron did anybody see, tiny tvs turned on from the planet?

It was obvious, for example, that Emma had watched a substantial portion of Aaron's first tour from the way she didn't just recognize rooms on the station (everybody'd seen the show at some point), but from how easily she placed him inside them: "Isn't that where you cut your finger that one time?" and "Hmm, you didn't put your dissection table there before." Just how much she had seen, Aaron didn't know and pretended he didn't want to. He actually wanted to know quite desperately (wanted to know how much she had watched him and why), but Aaron wasn't about to ask while the cameras were on and the cameras were always on.

Anything he said, Aaron'd learned the hard way, his wife might ask about back on Earth.

There was no real planet-to-station communication, although scientists did get rare messages from the surface, always from the producers of the show. One year, for example (the year before Aaron's first tour), they'd notified researchers that a pandemic was spreading across the Earth. The message was less to keep them updated (there was always some sort of disease, this in itself wasn't news) as to make sure they budgeted meals wisely, the network that financed the station not wanting touring scientists to starve, asking they recompute rations because they might be in space a little longer than they thought.

This, of course, set off a panic: The orbiting man (already a bit controlling) commandeered the female scientist's food, no longer trusting her to measure her own proportions, pressing himself against her body, shoving her against the wall. It was completely unprofessional (not just of the man, but of the producers to leave him there when he posed such a danger to the woman, pandemic now eradicated). But interactions like these kept the people on Earth watching, the ones who weren't friends and family that is (*panem et circenses*, and if the researchers who were on board couldn't grow the people bread, at least they'd get a show). The fact that they were orbiting the planet for a full year was what made it attractive to scientists.

After that, the producers started doing solitude testing, began better analyzing applicants before they accepted their applications. Aaron had rocked the isolation exam, performing better both scientifically and emotionally than any other candidate in the history of the program. (In addition to hidden cameras, Aaron highly suspected they were testing him, that psychologists and sociologists who watched the show used his behavioral data to form hypotheses of their own.)

Aaron was there for the unlimited funding (time) for experimentation, working to find some solution for the global fruit shortage. Here, he could see how berries reacted in the vacuum of space, whether microgravity environments accelerated or decreased their cycles of growth, playing with light and darkness, stressing and destressing every plant.

He's still that guy from college, Emma thought, watching now (together, in person). Are you able at all to pickup where you left off, she said. I thought the raspberry project you started your first tour showed remarkable promise, and Aaron just blinked.

I brought a few seeds, he said, setting out soil and fertilizer the first day.

This was going to be hard, finding a way to concentrate on his work without wondering how his wife might react to every interaction. She hadn't exactly been happy when he came home the first time, saying over and over, You didn't look like you missed me, sometimes you even looked happy, asking just what it was he'd been doing each time the camera was off.

I was in the bathroom, he'd said. Couldn't you tell from the footage that I went in, but still, she had her doubts.

That time, the other scientist and Aaron had scarcely interacted; Aaron barely spoke all year. (Do you have a family back home, he asked her one night, a husband, kids, and the woman just looked at him, terrified.)

But Emma was Emma (the same as she'd been in college): unadulterated lack of fear. He cautioned her every day the first month, No. I don't think you understand, pulling every bit of energy that he could away from his arms, trying to keep himself from brushing back her hair, people on Earth can see us, Emma whispering, You think I care?

You should. You've never been up here before, you don't understand (but how do you tell a butterfly its life lasts one season, Emma never thought about the long term of anything, at least she hadn't back in college, or maybe it was just she had nothing to hold her accountable down on Earth).

I'm going to live my life, Aaron, and my life just happens to be right here. If you don't want people watching, you shouldn't apply, and Aaron tried to tell her he hadn't come here to be seen, rather to get away.

I'm not one of those attention whores, she said, like, you know, the years where the people they send up here seem like the only reason they even became scientists was just to be on tv? I actually have things I want to do, an idea for a brand new pear tree, and then she shook her head. The maple, it just wasn't enough; I've got to bring back something people eat if I want to get anywhere back on Earth, and Aaron realized (in this way) Emma wanted to be seen, wanted the world to see exactly what it was she would do.

EARLY LOW BLUEBERRY
Left to its own devices, the vaccinium pennsylvanicum has a much longer harvest cycle than when intentionally cultivated. As Henry David Thoreau once wrote, "They ripen first on the tops of hills, before they who walk in the valleys suspect it."

The berry is small (no more than an inch in circumference), but by simply leaving the plant alone, it's (so far) become my largest harvest.

It started with collaboration (the nature of plants to interact), Emma and Aaron discussing how their projects could benefit each other. I'd love to learn more about the way fruit-bearing trees communicate, Aaron said. It's a shame we can't do cross-pollination experiments (the work section of the station not big enough, not to mention that required butterflies, wild bees). We all have to work within parameters.

It's nice, Emma said, being able to work beside you like this.

As undergrads, they'd never had the chance, occasional juniors winding up in senior classes, accelerated freshmen taking sophomore level. But never freshmen and seniors, no, the department only put all four years together for mixers (most students don't really begin networking until grad school, Emma's advisor had said, but with a personality like yours, you should take advantage). There were ice cream socials and picnics (or events that were called those things at least, liberal arts traditions running annums deep, still going in the twenty-third century, just without all that food).

Every time Emma went to a wine and cheese, she expected professors in houndstooth jackets (nineteenth century deerstalker hats, twentieth century elbow patches). They'd had wine, or a version of it at least, grapes gone soon after the berries, Sean joking that no matter what the universe threw at them, an enterprising student could still get drunk.

Wouldn't be college without it, he'd said, and in the corner, Emma saw Aaron was watching. He wasn't drinking anything, just holding a glass.

Aaron was leaning on the doorframe, analyzing everyone's

behavior and when he saw Emma looking at him, he stood up. (His body always shifted when she was around, feet and shoulders turning like branches.) For a moment, she thought he might come over, then her advisor walked up and said, You've made friends with Sean Gatling, I see.

And that was it as far as college. Those were the only two memories of Aaron she had. What she knew about him now was mainly from watching his tour: the way he rested each seed in the palm of his hand before planting, hovering over each hope-to-be plant in what looked like prayer. It wasn't studiousness, but reverence; Emma couldn't quite put her finger on it, but there was a motion, a regard. These berries were more than experiments to him, Aaron's approach more than science.

I like solving problems, he told her (week one, week two on station), Emma asking not why he chose to go back a second time, rather why he became a botanist.

Then why not computer science (Sean and his ilk having called themselves the problem makers, a coy team name pub trivia nights, saying if you want a real man to fix something, call a coder, a line so rote it was supposed to be a come-on, just one that didn't work on Emma).

I thought about it, Aaron said, turning on the overhead light. He leaned forward and looked at a blueberry seedling as though it were his child. I think this one might mature two days early, then reached for his notebook and jotted something down.

That's cute, Emma said and Aaron said, What, before thinking about his wife.

(She would be upset about this, he knew. As soon as he got home, she would ask, words spitting from her mouth like a mimeograph machine, Oh, and don't even get me started on that time she called you cute.

What did you expect me to say, he would ask.

I'd expect you not to flirt back.)

Your notebook, Emma said, it's cute. (Again, that word, Aaron working hard not to smile, straining muscles on his face.) Why don't you use the terminal, and Aaron answered, Why do you?

Well, she cocked her head, this is 2176. Where did you even get the paper (and looking up, again Aaron saw the camera, light's steady beam persevering).

Leave it to Emma to pick up on the one thing nobody else had (an entire year's research broadcasted from space and not a single other person had asked).

She wanted to know everything, asking question after question about his methods, not studying the berries he grew but mastering Aaron: why he did the things that he did, what it was that grew inside him.

I wonder, he thought, if she's this curious in bed, then looked at the camera again.

FLOWERING RASPBERRY
Progress! The earliest seeds are showing sprouts. I am watching them closely with hopes they will grow to full plant. Of the three that have emerged, two show signs of possible early yellowing (disconcerting), but at least for now they are growing. (For how long?)

You know I asked Sean about you once, she said and Aaron answered, What?

Back in college. I asked him to set us up.

Since when did you ever need anybody to set you up?

They were sitting at the table, Privacy Station laid out like a house (the dwelling part of it, that is): two bedrooms, shared bath, eat-in kitchen.

Freshman year, Emma said, or my freshman year, I mean. I asked Sean if he thought the two of us might work.

What'd he say, Aaron stirred oats in his reusable bowl, unwilling to look at Emma, afraid to look at the camera.

Oh, he said we'd be a complete disaster, setting her spoon to the side. He said you were too serious for me, that you weren't really there to have fun and that if I left you alone you'd make valedictorian. (He studies too much for you, Sean's exact words had been, and you need a man who enjoys a good time.)

I was, Aaron said. Valedictorian.

Well, there you go.

RED LOW BLACKBERRY (RUBUS TRIFLORUS)

Early flowering shows promise, as blooms transition to tiny berries. Right now, I'm looking at what Emma calls "a baby blackberry" the size of the nail on my little finger. It's a start. It isn't the raspberry yet (still anxiously watching that plant), but it's a start. Will it grow larger or should we count our blessings, knowing at least one missing berry has fully been reproduced? Is it realistic for a scientist to expect fruit yields the size that they were pre-Deadening on Earth?

It wasn't just the paper. Aaron did a lot of things the old-fashioned way, like washing dishes, something Emma had never done before. She'd always used the machine, the ultraviolet light ray system on board, put the dishes in (poof) they were done. But Aaron took his time, sudsing up soap and water, dipping his hands beneath.

At night, she would help. It was clumsy at first, Emma not sure what to do, Aaron handing her a cloth with a halfhearted smile, Here, you can dry, a concept that was foreign as well. He didn't dunk the dishes in the water as Emma had always imagined when she'd read about washing them in books. Instead, he placed them all in the bottom of the receptacle, then ran the water up. Taking another cloth, he would plunge his wrists and hands below the surface and move them. There was a friction to it, a certain type of light, eyes focused as intently on each dish as he did on his plants. Everything he does, Emma thought, he does well.

Don't drop it, Aaron said, handing her a glass. You just take it like this, hand sliding gently over hers, and move the cloth around, see? Now it's dry, then pointing, place it upside down over there.

Aaron was the same way with his work, having studied this technique a botanist tried in the late nineteenth century to measure and extend the dormancy stage of growth. Did you know, Aaron told her, that after London burned in 1667, wildflowers grew in its place? Plant seeds can be beautifully resilient, his whole face changing when he talked, and not just any flowers either, but ones people hadn't seen in years like London rocket and golden mustard. They'd been down there, waiting to grow that whole time. There was just a city in the way. Maybe what we need, Emma, turning the overhead off and placing his Iris scissors down, is simply to get out of the way.

According to Aaron, it'd been hundreds of years since anyone had tried cultivating plants with this method, a botanist named William Beal. In 1879, he buried 1,150 seeds in glass (you know we still haven't found all the bottles). A waste of resources, college Emma would have called it, but standing beside Aaron now, listening to him talk, it made her feel like maybe there was an advantage to moving backwards, something centuries of scientists overlooked.

The world's changed a lot, Aaron said, we don't know why the Great Berry Deadening happened. It could've been something new, yes, an action or chemical precipitating a major event. Or it could've been a decision people made centuries before you or I even walked the Earth.

(The butterfly effect, she said, and he nodded.)

Sometimes, I think it was a discovery that just went the wrong way. Like maybe people were trying to solve something, create a condition to grow more things, then poof, the berries were gone. Or maybe, just maybe (and with this, his features really came alive), the berries aren't dead, they're just waiting, and Emma thought, he's forgotten, the more he speaks the more he forgets and right now he's just talking to me, the cameras no longer exist, there's only him and me.

Even basics have to be questioned, Aaron said, arms stretched out before him, palms open. Shoots grow up, roots grow down; that's rule number one of plant life, right? But in space, what is up or down? They don't exist, they're arbitrary. Everything here is turned, and Emma wondered what Aaron had looked like as a child (afraid to let his intelligence show, was he laughed at).

Plants move differently here. They just do. Seeds remember their germination back on Earth. But the seeds that we planted here, they show an entirely different circumnutation, move in smaller spirals. Have you seen it with your trees? Everything comes around. Just look, taking a strawberry stem in his hand, see how it's curling? Plants do that naturally, toward light, but they don't go around and around like this; only in outer space. Everything here is full circle. Nothing is gone that can't be brought back.

Just think, Emma (smiling), What if we recreated the boysenberry? What if there are huckleberries or barberries or raspberries, just lying in wait down there? My God, Emma, do you remember raspberries? Or are you just younger enough than me to have never tasted one? Then taking her by the shoulders, Aaron said, They were amazing.

If I'm going to solve this problem, I have to trace it, look at the way things used to be, back when fruit was everywhere. Not just in microgravity environments, though: without pollutants or interference or whatever it was on Earth that caused the Deadening. It's like we're encased in glass up here. Whatever made them go away, Emma, it's down there, not here. Then gesturing to the tiny plants that grew all around, Aaron said, Here, this is where things grow, and Emma did not tell him there was no way to find bottles buried on Earth from outer space, no raspberry resurrection in sight. She just let him dream.

PASSIFLORA EDULIS
We have volunteer passiflora on station! A rare purple fruit that once grew in South America, I've only seen it in books, but Emma corroborates my findings. A passion fruit has indeed begun to grow at the base of one of her pear trees. According to my research, we should not expect it to fully ripen on the vine; once the fruit is ready for harvest, it drops.

Aaron did not mean to walk in on her in the bath. The living quarters were so small, anybody watching the show would never believe it, but she just lay in there so quiet, her body that night was so quiet, truly he did not mean to walk in on her in the bath.

POMEGRANATE
The one fruit I have planted that is not traditionally thought of as a berry because its husk has two skins, the pomegranate's classical associations remind us that our desire for fruit is more than a symbol of gluttonous temptation. With a ripe cycle both delicious and fleeting, it is the definition of beauty itself.

Aaron had loved his wife. Every man does at the beginning. But one day as he'd stood in their kitchen, holding contraband Ivory soap, he'd realized this wasn't just marriage, it was his life. They were in year three when it hit him: He'd wanted a union that was also a collaboration. It wasn't just that he'd finally been lucky enough to get a girl (botany was never a sexy science, as that asshole Sean Gatling'd pointed out), it was that Aaron got married because he thought marriage grew connection. This connection did not have to be his work, lots of married couples were in different fields, but Aaron's wife, well, she didn't work at all, doing interview after interview during Aaron's first tour, talk show after talk show about the strain of watching her husband orbit Earth with another woman. Then when he got back, for all of her questions, she never once asked did he like it, never once asked what he'd learned. She said he didn't look like he'd missed her, but question was, had she missed him?

So when Aaron got the chance to go back (producers calling, how 'bout it?), of course he'd said yes. Privacy Station provided unlimited time (space) for research, but better yet, he'd be alone. He could spend the entire year burying seeds and dividing them, no human (mis)connection to distract.

(But instead of being alone, he was alone with Emma. Here, he didn't just have a life, he lived it. Here, he was complete.)

They would have to go back (at some point the scientists always went back) but as he ran the dishwater now, as he looked over and saw Emma scraping their plates, she sat the cutlery down and he saw it, she lifted her hair and (again) he saw it: that tiny gray.

***

At night on Privacy Station, Emma played music to her trees, reaching out for Aaron's hand: Come dance with me.

FLOWERING RASPBERRY
If Charles Darwin was able to sprout 537 seeds from the mud he could fit in a breakfast cup, surely I can cultivate one worthwhile plant on the acre that is this station.

Under a microscope, things became clear. Not just the specimens (cell and molecule, nucleus and membrane) but life. Eyes above the lens, hands rotating the adjustment, Aaron could see anything clearly: Emma, his goal here on Privacy Station, life. And as he turned the aperture into focus, Aaron also saw his wife. She was there: an insect or aphid, tapping into the phloem to feed, injecting its virus cell, genome attacking each berry's DNA. Whatever he did, she would be there. It didn't matter what peace they'd found, how imaginedly perfect life with Emma could be. It was easy to forget now, sure, but one day, Aaron had to descend back to Earth. He could not live in the thermosphere forever, orbiting the planet below, and that's when he knew he had to tell her.

Emma, he whispered that night over dinner, eyes flicking up to the camera, can you come here, and when she leaned down, he whispered, told her something he'd never discussed his first or second tour, the part of his life he didn't want the world to know, and then when she stood, when Emma pulled away, he said, You know this means I could never leave her, then circled his beloved's wrist with the palm of his hand.

***

Lots of men could never leave their wives, that was the whole point of having one in a way. If men could leave, they'd just be girlfriends, there'd be no point in having a band, but knowing this didn't help anything, didn't keep Emma from crying harder as she lay day after day in her childhood bed back on Earth.

You've mourned enough, her mother said. I know it's hard. We all watched it. Honey, I was right up there in that station with you; there wasn't a moment I turned off that tv. But sweetheart, this lying around like this, crying all the time, it's not going to do you any good.

Why not, Emma asked. It's not like there's anyone watching. Why can't you just leave me alone?

FLOWERING RASPBERRY

Due to space limitations on station, I was forced to graft the one surviving plant too early. The result was a shorter, quite beautiful bush, but one limited in its capability to bear fruit. I have failed. They say there's no failure in science, only new discovery, but that isn't true. There may be hope with other raspberry species moving forward, but the rubus odoratus I adored as a child never will bloom again.

Emma had resigned herself to the fact that this was only for a season. She'd known before she left these were only one year tours. The producers sent two people at a time: a man and a woman. It wasn't uncommon for things to happen. (Scientists were not drones, they were people.) Put two like-minded people together in any close quarters and it would happen (he had never been alone, no matter how much solitude they wanted). Dating at work was frowned on among colleagues, but lots of botanists met during college then got married. Just because graduation and time now deemed them professionals didn't mean scientists no longer wanted sex.

And sex had been exactly what she was expecting. She'd seen enough seasons to know. There was always sex (some years, lots of sex). In fact, the only year Emma remembered watching where the tour hadn't ended with the researchers going at it like rabbits was the first year Aaron came. (She didn't know he could go again, nobody'd ever done that before. She'd never dreamed he would be the one on station.)

We're not doing anything wrong, she whispered, Aaron's body curled beside hers at night.

I'm not so sure about that, camera blinking (always blinking), and Privacy Station rolled on.

I GO TO PREPARE A PLACE FOR YOU

1. There are mai tais. I've never seen you with a mai tai, don't know what even goes in a mai tai, but the mai tais are there for me. They're there so you have something to make fun of me for, a brand new reason to laugh: *You concoct a dream world for me and don't bring bourbon? It's as if you don't know me at all* — but I do. I do know you and you love fruity drinks; you just won't admit it cause you're a man.

2. There are umbrellas. Not just the kind that go in your drink, right arm reaching even now toward the table to move the one in yours up and down (*see, I knew you'd love it* — you just shake your head), but the kind of umbrella we sit under: not to block the rain, but the sun. I like sitting in the shade and if you'll admit it, so do you. *We want to go to the beach*, I tell you, *but that doesn't mean we want a tan.*

3. There is the ocean. First and foremost, there is the ocean and if it weren't for the fact that you need to laugh so badly, baby this is where our story would have began.

4. There is no cancer. Nothing in my breasts, nothing in my lymph nodes, in my uterus or ovaries or anywhere else — no cancer in the world, anywhere. You don't have to fix me and, baby I don't want to fix you and there is no brokenness, no sickness anywhere.

5. You can sleep. You no longer wake, right arm reaching out to make sure that I'm still breathing. You no longer stretch your hand over the sheet to feel that it needs cleaning from the damp and the sweat that collect in the night, sickness of the chemo soaking through. There are no sheets on the beach, no beds to make,

they do it all at the hotel: 120 linen, 600 sateen and
when we lay down together, bodies healthy every
night, you tell me *this life is good.*

ESTHER

———

Now the king, he built him a palace and he named it Suzanne. Not that he knew any women named Suzanne, though the king, he did know women, and that's precisely why he named it that too. He could have chosen Susan or Ellen or Mary, but he'd already slept with women of those names, some names even twice, and he'd never met a woman named Suzanne. In other words, the palace name was one of hope.

Now the third year he was king, he held himself a dinner, inviting all the gentry and servants of the land, and not just his kingdom either, but from as far away as Paris and Malay. So they came, the people, all the people of all the provinces sitting and dining before him, from different countries, realms, and lands, and with the lot of them right there, he said this. Surrounded by jewels and riches and exotic animals, fruits and tapestries and linens, he said this.

But wait, he did not say it, at least he did not say it yet, telling the crowd to feast and drink, asking the queen Vashti to come closer. Each guest should drink his fill, but then they'd drink no more, for all must be done in accordance with the law. This was a palace of pleasure after all and if drunkness be your pleasure so be it, gold vessels and dark grapes pouring, but when he himself had gotten merry, he commanded that they stop. He commanded the seven chamberlains to stand in a circle around Vashti and look upon her, for she was so fair to look on.

But the queen Vashti, she would not be played, no, she wasn't one to be beckoned — or at least not anymore, tired of the king,

———

101

saying I've had enough of his crap, I don't live just to beck and come, I'm not doing this any more.

This of course humiliated the king, all the chamberlains and gentry staring, and his anger burned within him.

So the king, he said to the wise men, men who could see his anger piling like coins before him — well, this was when he said it, said out, we want her out, and the men knowing it was death to defy the king, well, the wise men all were pleased, saying defiance against one is defiance against us all and if we don't nip this in the bud, this and swiftly this, then all our wives will defy, think they and truly they have volition. And so the king, he said it: Get her out of our sight forever, never to come before us no more.

It wasn't death, but it was something, and the women were silently pleased. Sure, their lives wouldn't be much easier after this, masculine authority restored, but at least one of them, Vashti, at least she'd got what she wanted.

But you see, that made a new problem, meaning the king — while he did have women — was now without a wife. Being a philanderer was one thing (droit du seigneur and all that), but a whore was not a queen and if he were ever going to throw another banquet again, well, he needed somebody to show off.

So surveying the crowd and realizing that before him was all the land — men and women; boys and girls; gentry, servant, and slave — he thought, this is it. This is our golden opportunity. For you see, it would have been relatively easy for him to have ridden across his own kingdom, ridden across looking for a mate, fathers pushing their daughters out to be seen, dolled up in chiffon and lace. But this whole ordeal had been humiliating, the entire world had seen Vashti's rebellion, and so it was from the world he would take.

We will marry a new wife, he said, a new wife one year from today. So if you wanna be queen, ladies, line up. That's right, trot um out. For Vashti was known across the realms as most beautiful anywhere, but if you think your kingdom can do better, try us. So then the scribes handed him the scroll and upon it the king wrote this decree:

> To be published throughout all the
> lands, all the peoples, all the empires
> (but first, that is, our empire for our
> empire, it is great), our royal
> personhood doth seek a woman with
> beauty superior to that we have ever
> seen. Let fair, young virgins be sought,
> officers in each province appointed to
> seek them and gather the virgins up,
> line them in a row, a beauty pageant of
> sorts, with the winner getting to live in
> the palace.

Then thinking, the king did not put down his pen, rather looked out at the men. He looked at the chamberlains and he looked at the gentry, the wise men of Paris and Malay, and then he added

> Post-Script: All wives shall give honor
> to their husbands until the end of
> time; amen, [sic], &Cie.

Now outside the gates of Suzanne, there lived a woman named Esther. Wait, let's back up. First, there lived a man named Mordecai — son of Ya'ir who was son of Sam who was the son of somebody else and that guy was the son of Chris — and this Mordecai had a daughter, she was Esther. Mordecai and Esther were God's People.

The king did not like God's People; all people were his people, and no ruler — human, divinity, or otherwise — should ever come before him. But the decree clearly said "all the peoples," so unfortunately they had to be included (the king trapped in his own laws, you see) — or at least that's what Mordecai so aptly pointed out when he brought his daughter Esther unto Suzanne. Go with Hester, he said (because having both a Hester and an Esther in this story isn't at all confusing), go with Hester, Esther, and he'll take care of you. (Hester oversaw the pageant.)

So Hester lined her up and saw that she was fit — dark raven hair, strong arms — and passed Esther to the second round.

(If anyone ever asked Esther what she thought of this, what she had thought about anything at this stage at all, it didn't quite make it in the story. They didn't have our modern sensibilities back then, didn't think of women as more than chattel — but Esther, she wasn't chattel. She had her own thoughts, her own plans, and made much of them, just wait. Wait and you'll see that Esther isn't really being used in the way this part of the story makes it sound at all.)

Now by this point, Esther was already making friends in the palace, winning everyone over with her smile, growing more and more gorgeous by the day, skin soaking in six months' worth of myrrh oil, body lingering in vats, and the seekers and the servants and pretty much everybody in the palace secretly hoped that she would win. You see, even though they all hated God's People, Esther had never mentioned that she was one, Hester for some reason not telling nobody either.

(Maybe he was afraid he'd get in trouble, knowing how much the king loathed them, maybe he was secretly "GP" himself, or maybe — just maybe, the preachers preach — God worked on his heart despite his not being one of his People, for the benefit of those he loves, able to use those who don't believe in order to secure his People's protection.

Personally, I think he had the fear of Mordecai in him. Mordecai, every day, well, he stood at the walls of Suzanne, interrogating Hester about how Esther was getting on, a formidable man in wit and size.

Either way, it doesn't matter. It doesn't matter why Hester kept Esther's secret and the story, it moves along.)

Now when each maid had her turn, virgins on parade, the king sat bored in his chamber. He wasn't looking for traditional beauty, per se, but something different, the sort of woman you couldn't turn away from. Some, he kept for his concubinage, a white garden house in the palace backyard overflowing with myrrh, wild grapes, and sex. But the majority he sent home, back to their fathers like he did Vashti, not out of his sight forever, just, we thought we said no blondes, that one's overtly chubby, now get her away from we.

Then in the evening came Esther, after the king had enjoyed a lovely dinner, roast pheasant with wine; rosemary, sage, and shallots soaking in a sweet marinade; in other words, his belly was full. This one, he said, we'll keep her, then proclaiming himself delighted, deigned to ask Esther's name.

For you see, as I said, the king wanted something different and that, precisely, was Esther. Not because she was God's People — remember, nobody really knew this yet — but because she didn't wear any makeup. She didn't do her hair, just brushed it, parted it down the middle, and didn't put gold adornments on either. In all his life, the long and short reign of our mercurial king, never had he seen such resplendent beauty, never had a woman exuded this much confidence, standing silently before him while all the other contestants begged and clamoured. Let them go to the concubinage, he said, all those other women, but this one, this one delights us.

And that's how Esther became queen.

Now, while all this was going on in the palace, Mordecai was still dropping by the gates. He dropped by so often, in fact, he became a fixture, a fixture on the wall, heard but not seen, woodwork, dismissed, and that's how he heard the threat against the king. Let's take his life, one of the chamberlain whispered, bad man plotting in the dark, I'm tired of taking orders, off with his head this time, and when Mordecai heard that, well, he sent Esther a note.

An inquisition was made, Esther telling the king that the note was from Mordecai, a loyal and obedient servant to the crown, and looking into it, the wise men discovered he was right. Mordecai was right about everything, the wicked chamberlain and his friend plotting not just to kill the king, but also steal his crown. So then after both men were hung, the king took out his pen, took out his pen and wrote

> So shall Mordecai's name be forever
> written in the scrolls of gratitude.

Now, see, here's the thing: the chamberlain's death had created a job opening. The king was one man short. So he hired this guy named Haman, like hey, man, we've got a job over here, you want it? And as silly of a name as that may seem, Haman actually was good at his post, advancing quickly. In fact, before long, the king even gave him power of attorney, which sounds like a dumb thing to do if you're the king — giving away all your power — but really is quite pragmatic done right. Kingdoms are large and difficult to manage and if the king did any work, he'd have no time for leisure — and Suzanne, if you'll recall, was a pleasure palace.

And so Haman had the keys to the kingdom — or really not the keys but a writ of decree — and the first thing he did was require all people bow to him. Bow, you rabble, bow, don't kneel, seeing Mordecai had taken a knee, what are you doing, what even is that, slave?

Mordecai of course was no man's slave, but he didn't bother telling Haman that, knowing better than to pick a fight with a man of unchecked power, even if his daughter was the queen, so that's when he told Haman, I'll never bow to you, I'm God's People. (God's People, you see, well, they only bow to God, a fact commonly known through the land.

Now, you may be wondering at this point if the king knew that Mordecai and Esther were related and the answer is he did not. This was part of why Mordecai still stood at the gates, why every time he went to check on his daughter he didn't see her, passing messages and so forth through Hester, afraid that if the king did know they were related, he'd find out Esther was God's People, and who only knew what he'd do then.

As to how Esther herself got away without bowing, well, the laws of God's People didn't say be rude to the king, the exact opposite in fact, God encouraging those who love him to respect all edicts of man. But the rule was to have no gods before him and, in that day and age, bowing to something made it your god, at least in your heart if not in the mind, which left God's People fine making curtseys and kneels, and being a woman, Esther curtsied to the king every day.)

Anyway, Mordecai not bowing — and using religion to get out of it — made Haman so full of wrath and he thought to himself it'd be foolish, foolish to lay hands and crush Mordecai here, now, alone, for what would happen the next time Haman came upon one of these God's People who also refused to bow? So Haman sat in his heart to destroy the whole lot, to obliterate God's People from the earth, no more GPs now, no more GPs ever, and then Haman, he went to the king. He went to the king and said, your honor, sir, majesty on high, these people, you know who they are, God's People, they defy orders of the king, following not your ways but God's.

If it please, he then added — hoping very much that it would — let it be written that they're all to be destroyed and their property become the king's (knowing as power of attorney, he'd wind up with control over those funds himself).

And so the king took his hand and he pulled off his ring, took that ring and gave it to Haman. It is so, he said, ordering his scribes to bring in the scroll, where he wrote

> Haman has command over all our
> lieutenants and shall obliterate God's
> People from the land.

Here, the king said to the scribe closest by, write copies of this, one million copies — poor scribe looking down at his hand — and let it be known that God's People everywhere shall perish, be destroyed, the young and the old, even little kids. And our royal personhood demands all this done by Adar the 14th, "Adar" back then meaning March.

Now God only knows where Esther was all this time. Maybe she was in the bathroom, had stepped out for a walk, but needless to say she was not with the king. The queen did not just sit beside him all the time, no, she had her own things to do, but we do know where Mordecai was. He was outside the gates, and when he heard it, when he heard the wise men yell the decree, well, he rent his clothes (which is to say he ripped them), put ashes on his forehead, and cried.

After this, he tried to see his daughter — or maybe the king, I'm confused — but either way, the guards wouldn't let him in; no man can enter Suzanne undressed. So seeing how low he now was and in such a state, all of God's People except Esther, well, they ripped up their clothing too and fasted, wailing and mourning throughout the land. (Why not Esther, you ask, well, because at this point, remember, she doesn't know yet what happened.)

So finally Esther's maids come tell her, tell her Mordecai stood at the gates a-weeping. Then they told her why. And knowing she was God's People herself — that while the king did not know, she would not deny — Esther was afraid.

Send him fresh clothing now, she said, and then she called for Hester. Hester, she told him, the time has come whether you are God's People or not to stand beside us. As you know, whosoever shall come to the king in his inner court without invitation will be killed (which I guess is why Esther wasn't there when the king signed the edict, maybe she hadn't been invited that day). The only exception, Esther added, is if when you come, he holds out his scepter in sign that you might stay, and then the only answer Hester had for Esther was, Esther, you have to try, and that's when Esther knew, knew why her father had entered her into that silly pageant, why she became the queen.

Tell Mordecai, she said standing tall, to gather all of God's People, to crowd them near the walls of Suzanne, and to gird themselves in prayer. They shall neither eat nor drink for three days; in this, my maids and I will join them. When the fast is complete, I will go unto the king and enter his chamber — yes, I know it's against the law — and if I perish, I perish. But pray, dear Hester, that I live.

Now, it came to pass on the third day that Esther put on her royal apparel and stood by the inner court of the king and the king was upon his throne and, well, through the doorway he could see her, and as she was pleasing to his sight, he thrust out his scepter — a relief to young Esther indeed —saying, What can I do for my queen? And Esther did not say I want to live, you can change that silly law and make it where I might live; instead, knowing the king and how he loved his banquets, she said, come to dinner with me. And, if it pleases, bring Haman.

(Now, if you're anything like me, this is the point in the story where you're thinking if Esther is smart, she'll poison him, find a way to slip hemlock or something worse into Haman's food, be done with the buttmunch for all. But she doesn't. No, Esther invites them over to her rooms and they have a peaceable dinner instead, a very peaceable dinner, with shallots over rice and dates mixed with couscous, braised duck and roast geese and other savories. And when he'd had his meal, when the king'd had his full, he asked Esther, what do you want, babydoll? And Esther said, come back tomorrow night. Then Haman, walking home, thought heh, I'm gonna dine with the queen twice in a row, but soon his happiness left him, for stepping out from Suzanne, he saw God's People at the gates, praying in sackcloth and ashes, and then when he saw Mordecai with his righteous self, Haman's eyes narrowed into little slits and his heart hardened.)

That night, neither Haman nor the king was at all able to sleep (I swear Esther didn't slip anything in their food, not even caffeine), and while, in his insomnia, Haman planned a gallows fifty cubits high, well, the king desired to read. Bring us our scroll, he shouted, never perusing nobody's words but his own; then getting to the place with Mordecai's name — back when he'd saved his life and all — the king asked what was done for him, what was done for this man, besides being listed in the scrolls of gratitude, and when the chamberlains said nothing, the king, he said, well that doesn't sound real grateful to us.

So the next afternoon when Haman showed up for work, the king said to him, What shall be done for a man who delighted us, and Haman, thinking of course this was for himself, took a think. There had to be something, something befitting but not too outlandish, saying majesty, I've got it: Take your finest robes, well not really your finest but the next finest you don't wear anymore, and may royal apparel be brought to this man. Then your horse. The best in the stables, sit the honored upon it. And the crown, Haman slowly ventured — remembering the dead chamberlain but feeling on a roll — one of your extra crowns shall sit on his head; and then that's when he said it, when Haman finally said it: Proclaim to the whole kingdom that this is the man you choose to honor.

By Jove, the king said, we think he's got it. Get the clothes, wise men; run, chamberlain, run, get the horse. Come, Haman, we'll gather by the gates.

Well that Haman, he trotted himself out fine, smiling and grinning to all the folks and grinning even bigger when they got to the gates because there, there with God's People in ashes and rags prayed Mordecai — but then the king put the crown on Mordecai's head!

Needless to say that night Haman was still upset as he sat down to another dinner with the queen. What had he done to deserve this, baked chicken with balsamic dripping, what had he done to deserve this sort of treatment at all. It was embarrassing to stand there and watch Mordecai be praised. Haman couldn't even enjoy his candied walnuts. And just when you'd think Haman'd finally got his goose (when you think if Esther has them over one more time to eat), the king, well, he said, baby, just tell me what you want, and Esther said, I want to live.

What do you mean you want to live, you're living now, and it took a while to get the king to shut up, for he wasn't a man to listen, Esther laying it out like this: I am God's People and we are to be destroyed. Were we naught but sold to slavery, I would have held my tongue, for as a woman I know I am never truly free. But we are not. We are to be killed. And I want to live.

Then the king, well, you'd have thought he didn't know a thing about it, not a thing about it at all (and maybe he'd forgot, the mercurial thing, and that's why he had Haman, why he'd needed a power of attorney to begin with, because how could one king keep up with every little thing) but (whether he did or he did not remember), he sure was angry about it now.

Who did this, said the king, where is he who presumes so? And Esther reached out her hand and pointed.

Now the king, he had a problem, see, specifically that while it was very very easy for him to enter decrees into law, it was not so easy to undo them, asking the scribes to bring back the scroll, so even though the whole thing had been Haman's idea, the law was still the law.

(Meanwhile Haman, he was a-groveling, groveling with a little spot of grease by his mouth, having had the unfortunate timing of biting into buttered lambtail right when Esther'd spoken — or pointed with her hand, I mean, but either way, the situation wasn't good for him, for the king took back his ring and, on that very night, hung Haman, hung him by the neck in the gallows he'd made for Mordecai, a justice some say is sweeter than cobbler with berries.)

Or was it? Haman wasn't king and never had been, so as to whether anything he'd done was or was not law, well, that part maybe was debatable. He'd been power of attorney, power of attorney and nothing more, and the only evidence of that was the ring. What is written, can it be unwritten, Mordecai ventured to ask, patience and prayer having brought him this far, for if the king is mighty, can the king not trump himself?

Who in all the lands is more powerful? Who are men to say this is written, who are they to stake the law? Would a strong king endure such pain upon people, kill and slaughter children, overruled by a technicality? Nay, my King — meaning God's People's God, the King of all Kings Himself — my King is greater than this.

So the king called his scribes, chamberlains, and wise men, and made them haul the scroll back to his chamber (weary, they were, from all this toting, it was the third time they'd brought it that month), and then he made a new law, much better than the old:

> God's People shall not be killed and
> Mordecai shall be their captain,
> captain being higher than a lieutenant
> but not a ruler,

(for the king learned his lesson last time, no powers of attorney any more)

> having authority but not reign over
> God's People from Harriet to Cush:

(Harriet being the old palace, the one abandoned for Suzanne)

> in all 127 provinces, each and every
> one to be given its own scroll,
> translated into whatever language it is

those people speak, so that all may
know we're still the king, he is just a
captain.

And the young scribe again looked at his hand, looked down at his hand and felt weary, but he wrote all those copies, translated them nonetheless, and over horseback, they were delivered. Then in every province, all of the cities, all of the towns, wherever the Word it came, God's People had joy and gladness, joy and gladness and roast duck with cherries, a feast and a very good day.

And Esther (in case you forgot about her, because admittedly, she is in the background a lot for this to be her story), well, Esther asked that Haman's sons be hanged, not just enough to have him gone, but desiring all Haman's line be obliterated from the earth, (and if you think that sounds cruel, well, it is. Had his sons done anything to her? Why, their being his sons was no different from God's People being born into their families, wanting to kill somebody for the accident of their birth. But maybe they were mean or maybe she knew them after all and that just didn't make it in the story — or maybe, just maybe this part is there to prove that even if they were God's People, they were still just people, and Haman did try to kill her father after all, so who wouldn't get mad over that? But either way the moral is the bad guy(s) died and God's People lived and) you never know quite when the Lord will use you. You never quite know what you'll be. Something can seem horrible, things can look real bad, but there is a plan, there is a story, and maybe one day you kids'll tell your story to me.

TELL ME WHAT YOU SEE

"Alright, Lily. This isn't going to hurt," Dr George spun the phoropter around, bending it toward the little girl's face. It wasn't uncommon for children to recoil at the device, intimidated by its many lenses and knobs, so he tried to unfold it as slowly as he could.

"It's a mask," he used to say, "like Halloween," encouraging the children to choose their own monsters: an octopus, an insect, a bee. That, he thought, had been a novel idea, Dr George even sharing it with colleagues at conferences, sitting at the hotel bar, chatting about pediatric care. But then he'd read in the National Journal of Behavioral Ophthalmology that this could actually scare children more, poor little things' imaginations running wild, so he'd decided not to do that anymore. He wouldn't overexplain (they were kids, after all) but he would no longer be coy, mask language gone, saying "It won't hurt, I promise" instead. Children always understood a promise.

"I'm going to use a chart," he explained, "In a minute, I'll put it up on the wall. And you lean forward here," gesturing for the little girl to rest her forehead in the center of the machine, "look through these holes,"  , "and tell me what you see."

Dr George motioned toward his assistant, Matilde. "Would you like my friend to sit beside you?" and Lily nodded.

"Okay," he said, "Now don't be afraid. I'm going to have to turn the lights down a little," using a dimmer on the wall, "but there's nothing to be concerned about. Just be honest, and tell me what you see," then he flicked the examination chart on.

"**E**," the child started to read, "**F** **P**

," Dr George sitting back, flush in his chair, "**T**," and as she continued, he looked at Matilde.

"Stop. Stop, sweetheart, now please," looking at Matilde to see her face had gone white, Dr George taking a breath, not sure what to say. "Are you telling me you see letters?"

She nodded.

"Okay," said Dr George, "Let's try this again," twisting and turning knobs and dials, adjusting prisms and axes with his hands. "Let's try this one more time."

E F P
T O Z

" E ," she said, " T O Z ."

"No," he said firmly, "stop," not liking his own tone, realizing as the words came out how harsh he sounded, how harsh he must sound to a child. He couldn't hide the fact that something was wrong, but he didn't want to scare her. He couldn't see it in her eyes (the fear), but he could see it in her face.

Beside the little girl, Matilde had begun to shake, ever so slightly folding her right fingers around her left hand, pressing her thumb into her palm. He was going to have to speak with her again. She was there to be a comfort to the patients, to make the children feel less alone, and in interview, she'd seemed perfect for the job. "There's no greater gift than the ability to see," she'd told Dr George and from the tone in her voice, he knew she meant it. This wasn't just a job to her (or for that matter, to him). She cared about their patients, especially the children, and these days they were always children.

This, for the most part, was thanks to the government. Partnering with the national educational system, federal health had gotten much better at catching citizens' vision needs early. As a result, there were rarely fully-grown adults in need of correction, most patients visiting the eye doctor by the end of first grade, teachers catching their vision difficulties when they asked too many questions, noses pressed, shoulders bent above the page. Once you got to that age, it was impossible to function without normal sight.

Lily was barely five, flagged her first full week of kindergarten, red tab on her folder indicating the teacher thought hers was an extreme case. But there'd been nothing in the child's medical or school history to indicate how extreme, as Dr George looked back over at Matilde.

Matilde really was doing her best, it was easy to see, continuing to press that thumb down into her palm, use reflexology, to breathe. But the caring that had stood out in her interview (an obvious compassion, the woman's empathy clear-cut) sometimes could do her in, internalizing the patient's inability to see. It would burn her out if she didn't watch it. As professionals, they couldn't focus on how hard these kids' lives had been (physically fumbling their way through life, eye strain and headaches not ceasing), they had to focus on each correction.

"Abnormal," his assistant whispered (in her left canthus, a small tear forming), "You poor, poor child."

Yes, thought Dr George, we definitely need to speak about this later.

"Sweetheart," he said, proceeding with the exam (the only real thing he could do), "can you tell me the smallest thing you see?"

" P E Z O L C F T D ," she read, letter after unexpected letter, and Matilde was not the only one concerned.

Patients who saw characters and graphemes were not complete unknowns. In med school, Dr George's professors had taught that in the early days of behavioral ophthalmology (back before government care), correctors had used a different chart than they did today — something called a Snellen. He'd never seen one personally, but they allegedly had looked the way Lily described, a gigantic E at the top with gradually smaller letters descending in rows, each row indicating a different capacity for normal vision.

In a way, the concept was not unlike the chart they now used, an image normal vision perceived as everyday (as common as sunlight or trees). Like the Snellen, it too had its larger and smaller features: the tinier the details a patient could see, the greater their visual perception. "Modern charts are much more precise," his med school professors had taught them, "allowing us to fine tune corrections for an even more perfect sight." Thanks to the government's new image-based model, correctors could pinpoint a patient's axis down to one-fourth of a degree. The only reason the Snellen was even remembered today, his professors explained, was because "It's where the expression 20/20 comes from — what can the patient see from twenty feet."

So occasionally, before the educational system partnership (back when Dr George was early in his career), a corrector would get an older patient who'd maybe been told about the Snellen, had heard stories from their grandparents in their youth ("when I went to the doctor, he had me read off the wall"), and those patients sometimes tried telling Dr George they saw letters, their vision so bad (in deep need of correction) that their eyes couldn't accept the image whatsoever and they told him what they thought they were supposed to see in order to pass the test. But these patients didn't see letters. Not really. If someone looked at the chart and saw letters, they couldn't perceive normal at all.

"Sweetheart," Dr George spoke carefully, thinking around every word. This was a school child, in kindergarten, a young girl learning to read. She was far too young to have heard of the Snellen, but that didn't mean she wasn't imagining things. He had corrected many children with a surplus of imagination, who told him they saw the ghost of letters (their shapes slightly grayed, haunting the chart). They were the dreamers, people who wanted to see more so they did (something that looked like an E, "there at the top of the chart," the crown of the dome a little jagged, pareidolia).

Maybe that was it. Maybe the little girl was envisioning letters, maybe she was trying to please. "I need you to look one more time for me," he said, "Is there anything else you can see?"

"What do you mean?" she asked, so he pulled up the test again:

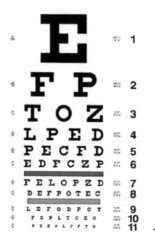

"Around those letters you mentioned. Or outside them," Matilde holding back more tears, "Is there anything else?" Lily's eye lenses refracting in time, Dr George pleading. And as the child began to describe numbers, actual digits descending down the side, Dr George thought this is bad, this is very bad indeed. "Alright," he said to Matilde, motioning toward the cupboard, "Time to get the drops."

Matilde's eyes grew wide as she reached down in the drawer beside her and took out the cabinet key. The child wasn't that afraid before (not like other children had been), but if his assistant kept crying she was going to be. "Matilde," Dr George said (face and hands pantomiming, feigning the motion of tears), then he shook his head.

"Sweetheart," he told the little girl, "this is all going to be okay. I promise. What you're seeing here, well, it isn't what kids are normally supposed to see. But the good news," nodding again at Mathilde, "is that we're going to get you fixed up right away," then asked Matilde to lean back the chair.

"Alright," folding the phoropter away, Dr George gently leaning toward the child, "we just need you to keep your eyes open for one," squeezing the bottle, "and two," sulfur and atropine dripping, "Now one more time," he squeezed again, "and just like that, we're done! Now see," pulling his body back with a smile, "that wasn't hard at all."

Lily blinked, black pupils in the center of both eyes expanding, "What did those do?"

"It's called dilatation," Dr George told her, "We just opened your eyes up a little bit to make it easier to look inside them. Does it hurt?" and when the little girl told him no, he said, "See, I told you it would be okay," then patted her knee before folding the phoropter back in front. "Alright. What a good girl. Now lean forward for me one more time and tell me what you see."

Then Lily, she repeated the same letters as before, saying this time

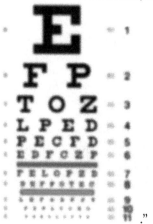

they were a little blurry: "   ."

"Blurry how," asked Dr George, "as in you can't really see them or like they're obscured —," Matilde interrupting, saying "Smoke;" Dr George shaking his head, "Is there anything else?" and Matilde whispered, "No people?"

"No," Lily said.

The smarter the child, the worse the sight, according to multiple studies. The science didn't go back as far as the Snellen, but the link between intelligence and vision was long accepted fact. In certain cases, yes, the physical shape of the eye itself made a difference, astigmatism caused by an imperfect cornea that curved in one direction on the right side, another on the left — or myopia, for example, where the eyeball was too long. But the degree of the problem, how severe any particular vision problem was or was not, that was principally intelligence related, receptors in the occipital lobe processing light and color, sight more dictated by the brain than by the eyes. It took a very smart mind to realize it couldn't see, to perceive abnormal vision. And this little girl, Dr George thought, was a very bright child indeed.

"We're going to give something new a try, okay, sweetheart?" and then leaning forward (toward the dials and toward the child), he flipped three lenses on the right. "I need you to tell me if you can

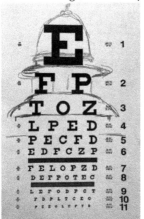

see better one," , turning another

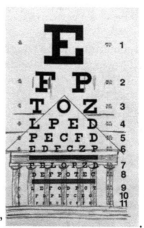

dial, "or better two,"   .

Lily bit her lip. "The first one, maybe?" (thinking at least then she could see more letters), and Dr George sat back, relieved.

"Astigmatism," he said, giving Matilde a confident look. "I knew it."

"How can you tell?" she asked and Dr George explained, "The curvature. The first correction brings it out more," then crossing his arms, he leaned back and thought.

"Alright, sweetheart, I'm going to change us back to number one, okay?" adjusting the dial. "I'd like you to look again," moving out of the way so he didn't block the chart, Dr George said, "Now tell me what you see?"

"The letters," Lily said, "They're all still there. But," squinting her eyes and taking a pause, "there's this little drawing on it now," describing where it stopped and started:

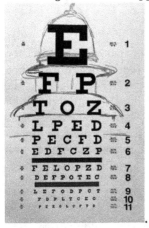

Dr George was at a loss. "The drawing," he said, "is it more or less clear than the letters?

What does it look like?"

"I don't know. A bell?"

"Thank God," Matilde said, "She can see the dome," picking up Lily's hand, "Don't worry," holding her remaining tears back, "When I was your age, I needed correction too."

"That's very kind," Dr George told Matilde, "Can you go in the lobby please and update her teacher for me?" then leaning over his desk, wrote out one single word, turning the notepad where only Matilde could see:

"S U R G E R Y."

"Is it covered?" Mathilde asked.

He nodded yes.

Years ago, early in Dr George's career, he had made the decision to only take patients who were on the federal health insurance. It wasn't altruism (caring for the poor), rather foresight. At the time, his colleagues had scoffed at the decision, questioning Dr George's judgement at conferences, saying they were glad somebody at least was willing to work for what the government paid, but that person wasn't about to be them: "You'll regret it in the end." But he had not. A couple of administration changes and a massive societal shift later, and by the time Dr George had reached his forties, eye exams were mandated by the state.

It made sense if you thought about it: People couldn't drive, assist others, walk down the street, it's amazing the list of activities in the public sphere where everyone needed to see. Want to get your license? Better pass that eye exam. Receive federal benefits? Same. It was ludicrous what people before had tried to do with abnormal vision. Eyesight affected executive function, the ability to focus. It had to come to an end, this part of the population that could not see. It was dangerous. Take voting for example (how frightening that had been), to think people used to be able to go in a booth and tick a box without even proving they could clearly perceive the ballot.

For mankind, the correction requirement had created a better society; for Dr George, it made a livelihood. In order to ensure wide-scale adoption, Uncle Sam had built off of its existing healthcare plan, refusing to accept eye exam results from doctors who weren't in network. And all those colleagues who once had scoffed, had their fun at Dr George's expense, well, many of them had gone into early retirement. Some had joined the system, sure, their practices operating on a shoestring as case workers and teachers who referred pediatric patients kept sending children to Dr George, a corrector they'd already trusted for so many years.

I've helped a lot of kids in my time, Dr George thought, and I'll get this one seeing normally too.

In the corner, Matilde reentered, closing the door as quietly as she could. Dr George whispered, "So?" and she nodded yes and Dr George said, "Alright, sweetheart. Let's see."

"Your eye is the wrong shape," he told the child, remembering his pledge to the truth, "Most kids, their eyes are like baseballs — rounded in the front. Yours are like footballs and that's keeping your mind from accepting what your eyes should be accustomed to," the latter flying over the child's head completely (little girl now starting to be afraid). "Matilde, if you would hand me the microkeratome, please," and as his assistant flicked it on, a slight buzzing filled the room.

"Okay. Here's what we need you to do, sweetheart. Matilde is going to be right here. She's going to hold your hand. But I do need you to keep looking at that chart while I operate, okay? Just keep looking right up there and tell me what you see," lowering the metal cylinder to compress Lily's anterior chamber and lens.

"Just the letters with the thing on top," she told him while

Matilde patted her hand. "Wait," lenses and corneas partnering

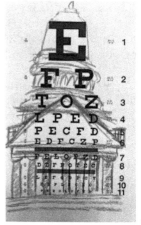

together, light passing to the retinas," ."

"That's fantastic," Dr George said, "I am so proud of you," while he sliced the top of her corneas off, creating a tissue flap.

"Hang in there, Lily," Matilde told her, "Me and Dr George'll have you fixed up in a jif," Dr George asking how many columns she could see, if the columns all had capitals ("that's what you call the part on top"), and when Lily said yes, he asked her to describe their shape.

"Wait," she said, Dr George manipulating her corneas, folding away the tiny flaps, "I see people. They look like little dots

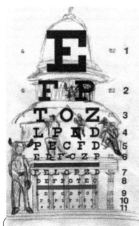

() crawling up the side," biting her lip again. "I — I don't think this is right," she said, Dr George trying to persuade her those men were supposed to be there, "There's one with horns. Like a bull. And he's holding a flag?"

"Where is it," Dr George asked, "the flag? Can you see more than one?" and at first she told him no, but then,

"Very good," he told her and even Matilde mustered a smile, tears starting to dry as she slightly released the tension with which she'd been holding Lily's hand.

"We just need you to hang in there a little longer," Dr George said, "You're doing very well," pulsing corneal tissue with a laser, lowering the flaps back down, "Just a few more tweaks."

"Watch it, kiddo," Matilde leaning in, stopping herself from brushing back Lily's hair, "When all of this is over, you'll see just like any other kid," the child's sight coming more into focus,

more people and then more flags, and that's when Lily started crying (sodium and lysozyme falling, blue mucin bleeding forth). "She's so happy," Matilde said, "Just look, Dr George. How happy she is to see!" but as the chart came more into focus, corrective surgery now complete, the letters, they all went away, and Lily screamed:

"This isn't normal. Matilde, help me!"

"What?" Matilde said, releasing Lily's hand, "What do you mean?" gesturing toward the chart with both arms, "This is exactly the way it's supposed to be."

But Lily, she kept on blinking, lenses clouding over as her pupils dilated with light, occipital lobe still fighting, grappling with the sight. Dr George turned off the microkeratome, the phoropter he put away, then leaning toward his patient, he asked, "Now tell me what you see."

Acknowledgments

Writer: Terena Elizabeth Bell

Publisher and editor: Miette Gillette

Alpha and beta readers of individual stories: Anonymous, Lisa Beth Bell, Terry Bell, Janie Bradshaw, Rebecca Conley, Laura Gilbert, Bill Glass, Adele Glimm, C.S. Hanson, Faith Miller, Nancy Novick, Andrew Shaffer, and Karen Wunsch

"Welcome, Friend," was first published in the March 2022 issue of *streetcake*.

An interactive version of "#CoronaLife" (including gifs in lieu of still images) was published June 29, 2022 by *Boudin*, the online home of the *McNeese Review*: https://www.mcneese.edu/thereview/2022/06/29/coronalife-by-terena-elizabeth-bell/

The title story, "Tell Me What You See," was written in honor of Congresswoman Haley Stevens and all others who champion democracy. Keep going.

"Tell Me What You See" was also a 2021 New York Foundation for the Arts City Artist Corps winner. Together with additional support from the New York City Department of Cultural Affairs, the NYC Mayor's Office of Media and Entertainment, and Queens Theatre, this grant funded a free, public performance of select stories from this book with other work on September 21, 2021 in Manhattan. The following individuals made the evening go smoothly: Edward Babbage, Davis Cherry, and Alexander Sorokin, as well as host site staff and multiple attendees.

About the Author

Terena Elizabeth Bell has written for more than 100 publications, including *The Atlantic, Playboy, Yale Review,* and others. Her short fiction has won grants from the Kentucky Foundation for Women and the New York Foundation for the Arts. *Tell Me What You See* is her first collection of short fiction. Originally from Sinking Fork, Kentucky, she lives in New York.

Learn more at terenabell.com.

About the Publisher

Whisk(e)y Tit is committed to restoring degradation and degeneracy to the literary arts. We work with authors who are unwilling to sacrifice intellectual rigor, unrelenting playfulness, and visual beauty in our literary pursuits, often leading to texts that would otherwise be abandoned in today's largely homogenized literary landscape. In a world governed by idiocy, our commitment to these principles is an act of civil service and civil disobedience alike.

CPSIA information can be obtained
at www.ICGtesting.com
Printed in the USA
BVHW060452170223
658647BV00006B/420

9 781952 600227